Strebor Quickiez

What is a Strebor Quickiez? Years ago, I decided that I wanted to create a series of short, erotic books that would be designed to be read in the span of one day. Thus, the Strebor Quickiez collection was born. Whether a reader takes in the excitement on the way to and from work on public transportation, or during their lunch break and before bedtime, they can get a "quick fix" in the form of a stimulating read.

Designed to be published in collections of three to six titles per season, Strebor Quickiez will be enticing to those who steer away from larger novels and those who do not have the time to commit to spend a longer span of time to take in a good read. The first set includes *The Raw Essentials of Human Sexuality*, *One Taste* and *Head Bangers: An APF Sexcapade*; the follow-up to my wilder successful novel *The Sisters of APF: The Indoctrination of Soror Ride Dick*. Rounding out the collection is a trilogy featuring three women who receive separate invitations to make their respective sexual fantasies come true: *Obsessed*, *Auctioned* and *Disciplined*.

It is my hope and desire that booksellers embrace Strebor Quickiez and promote them to their consumer base. I am convinced that these books can do a heavy volume in sales and, as always, I appreciate the support shown to all of my efforts throughout the eight years.

Blessings,

Zane

Also by Allison Hobbs

Pandora's Box

Insatiable

Dangerously In Love

Double Dippin'

The Enchantress

A Bona Fide Gold Digger

The Climax

Big Juicy Lips

ONE TASTE

A NOVEL

ALLISON HOBBS

SBI

STREBOR BOOKS
NEW YORK LONDON TORONTO SYDNEY

Strebor Books
P.O. Box 6505
Largo, MD 20792
http://www.streborbooks.com

This book is a work of fiction. Names, characters, places and incidents are products of the author's imagination or are used fictitiously. Any resemblance to actual events or locales or persons, living or dead, is entirely coincidental.

ISBN-13 978-1-59309-178-1
ISBN-10 1-59309-178-8
LCCN 2008941725

First Strebor Books trade paperback edition February 2009

Cover design: www.mariondesigns.com
Cover photograph: © Keith Saunders/Marion Designs

10 9 8 7 6 5 4 3 2 1

Manufactured in the United States of America

This book is dedicated to

Charmaine Parker

You are a true blessing in my life.

Thank you for the years of encouragement, kindness, and friendship.

ACKNOWLEDGMENTS

The Strebor *Between The Sheets* Tour Divas: Marsha Sanders, Suzetta Perkins, and Tina Brooks McKinney. I'm honored to share the adventure with the three of you.

Keith Saunders (Marion Designs): Thank you for yet another unique and steamy cover.

Jessica Holter…Sexy genius. I'm thrilled to collaborate with you.

Karen Dempsey Hammond. Can't pick family but I can sure pick my friends. You are my sister, my soul mate, my best friend.

Aletha Dempsey. Yeah, you're grown. But you're still cute as a button.

Korky & Shari…I'm so proud of you two. Keep it up.

ZANE, take a bow! As you continue to make history, I'm smiling and applauding in a perpetual state of awe.

CHAPTER 1

Regina Wheeler brushed her hand against the expensive bronze metallic leather clutch and shivered as instant euphoria coursed through her body. Designer handbags, clutches, totes, and shoulder bags were her passion—an obsession of monumental proportion. She could eye spy a knockoff with just a glance. Her designer collection hung on the backs of three of her closet doors, were stacked in boxes on shelves inside closets and drawers in the spare bedrooms, and there was even a secret stash in the basement.

She couldn't resist fondling and inhaling the soft leather once more before paying for the stylish clutch.

Unfortunately, she wouldn't have the luxury of putting her latest acquisition on display in her bedroom where her eyes could feast upon it. Not wanting to hear the words "Another expensive bag?" from her husband's lips, Regina would have to conceal her purchase. This new beauty would have to be hidden in the basement with the rest of her prized possessions—dozens of colorful bags covered with protective plastic.

And when she decided to carry the metallic clutch, Matt would roll his gaze to the ceiling. "Is that new?" he'd ask suspiciously. Regina would reply ever so innocently, "No, honey. I bought this last year." He'd frown and mumble in dissatisfaction, but her denial would quash an endless sermon about frivolous spending and how they needed to tighten their budget. At that point, Regina would solemnly agree to cut back on spending and the bronze metallic clutch would join the other beautiful bags displayed in their bedroom.

At home, Regina clicked on the basement light and bounced down the stairs. One of these days she and Matt were going to invest in getting the basement remodeled to give it a finished look—add a powder room, plasma TV, pool table, the works. Matt always complained that if it weren't for all the money Regina spent on her obsession the basement could have been refinished years ago.

She stood for a second at the cedar closet, ran her hand across the surface in reverence. Treasured possessions that had belonged to her son—his favorite toys and items of clothing that she'd cherished and was unable to part with—were stored inside the cedar closet, which was kept padlocked.

She kept her collection inside that sacred place, also. It was a good hiding place; her husband would never go snooping inside the cedar closet. Too many painful memories were locked within.

In fact, her husband hardly ever descended the basement stairs. He didn't have the time to fiddle with the manly tools and gadgets that occupied the basement. Working a full-time job, running a business, and training employees was more than enough work for one man, he'd told his wife. So Regina, finding herself unable to fit another item inside the cedar closet, figured she could hide the narrow box containing the bronze clutch in the storage area where her husband kept his neglected tools.

She rearranged some of the gadgets and pushed the box to the back of the shelf where it would be undetected. Though the box was small, she couldn't push it out of view; something was in the way. Standing on her tiptoes and stretching her arm as far as she could, she used the tips of her fingers to retrieve a package that crinkled as she pulled it out of its hiding place.

It was a shiny bag with a T-Mobile logo. Regina snatched open the bag. Curious and slightly disturbed, she scrutinized the packaged cell phone. The state-of-the-art device came equipped with internet access and a host of features. Matt must have intended to give the phone to his seventeen-year-old nephew, Eric.

Regina frowned in thought. Matt had already given Eric a cell phone. Granted, the manufacturers came out with newer models at a rapid rate, but she and Matt didn't make the kind of money required to keep up with modern technology. She was surprised that Matt, usually frugal to the point of being obnoxiously stingy, would go behind her back and secretly give his nephew a more expensive, upgraded model. Sure, Eric was his favorite nephew but it wasn't as if he were their own son.

Our son. Regina's eyes watered instantly. Her little boy—her baby—would have been close to Eric's age now. He'd be in high school. She wondered how he'd look—how he'd behave as a teen. Would he have remained as sweet, as good-natured as he'd been as a child? Frowning, she shook her head, trying to rid her mind of painful memories. But it was too late—images of her little boy's face began to flash like a fast-moving slide show.

"*Devon*," she cried aloud as she was hit by a pang of yearning so severe it was almost disabling. Clutching her heart, Regina slumped against the storage bin.

Though she was alone in the house, Regina wept quietly. Her tears, like her designer bags, were kept secret. Crying over a son she'd lost ten years ago was considered unhealthy. "Life goes on," well-meaning friends had told her.

Life goes on? Maybe so for other people. Even Matt had found a way to cope. He seemed to have replaced Devon with his nephew, Eric. He played surrogate father to Eric, participating in all his academic and sporting events. Regina was fond of Eric but she couldn't bring herself to dote on him as Matt did. It seemed unfair to Devon.

It took an hour for the sobbing session to end and when she finished crying, feeling purged, she straightened her shoulders and dried her eyes. She glanced at the T-Mobile package and shrugged. She'd pretend she didn't know about the phone and wait until Matt was ready to reveal why he felt the need to indulge Eric with yet another hi-tech phone.

Matt had been employed at Boeing Helicopters in Ridley Park, Pennsylvania, since he was eighteen years old and right out of high school. Now, a year shy of his fortieth birthday and feeling that life was passing him by, Matt had invested his life's savings and had even taken out a loan, for which Regina had co-signed, to start a commercial cleaning business. He had a staff of four—three men and one woman—all recovering substance abusers.

Every evening at five-fifteen, Matt pulled up in his van and picked up the foursome on the corner of Ninth and Central Avenue in Chester, Pennsylvania. From there, he transported them to various commercial businesses in the tri-state area, where they were on a tight schedule to get the work done and then move on to the next building.

He usually dragged back home around midnight and was up again at six in the morning to start his day job at Boeing. It was grueling, but having his own business gave him a sense of purpose and seemed to brighten his life.

Though Regina had little faith in Matt's ability to succeed in the cleaning industry his renewed zest for life was worth every dime of their joint life savings that he'd sunk into the business. She could sleep easily at night because her pension at her job as a marketing manager at an insurance company, as well as her 401K account, were the back-up plan.

With Matt working such long hours, Regina's life had become a little more tolerable. The best part of having a husband who worked sixteen hours a day was that he was too exhausted to harass her at night. Well, at least not as often as he used to. For the first few years of their marriage Regina—having had only one sex partner in her life—thought Matt's undersized penis was normal.

Early in their marriage when sparks didn't fly, she'd hoped that in time and with a little more experience, their love life would escalate to hot and steamy instead of remaining lukewarm. And boring. He'd been a premature ejaculator from the beginning of their marriage, but Regina had learned to accept that as well.

It took two years for her to even admit to her husband that she'd never achieved an orgasm. He looked at her with utter shock. "Why not?" he asked accusingly as if there was something wrong with her. The sudden tension in the atmosphere caused Regina to back down. Sparing her husband the humiliation of being told that his equipment as well as his bedroom skills were lacking, Regina mumbled that she didn't know why she had never reached a climax. Protecting her man's ego, she took the fall, which resulted in the unspoken conclusion that she, and not Matt, had a problem.

Over the years, Matt did nothing to improve their sex life. He continued to rush through foreplay and never bothered to experiment and find her pleasure points. After one sloppy kiss, he'd run his hands impatiently over her breasts, squeeze her thighs, and then penetrate. After a few thrusts, he'd ejaculate. His body would jerk spastically. He'd groan so loud and for so long, Regina often feared that neighbors would think Matt was being attacked by a violent intruder and consider it their civic duty to call 911. With all that post-intercourse commotion, one would have thought Matt had been stroking her long and hard.

Now he had a new dysfunction. In addition to being undersized and prone to pre-ejaculation, Matt could not maintain an erection. He'd urge her to "play with it." And when her half-hearted hand job failed to keep him hard, he'd straddle her, rub his little dick on her tits, turn her over, and try to stuff it between her buttocks. When he finally became semi-erect, he'd quickly turn her over on her back and pant like an animal as he desperately tried to force himself inside her. His semi-erect dick would slip out of her opening and Matt would quickly, desperately, stuff it back in.

She supposed her husband's dick problems had desensitized her. Since he couldn't deliver the goods, it would seem the decent thing to do would be for him to go on about his business and leave her alone. Sex with her husband had become worse than just an unpleasant chore. It was torture.

Until six months ago. That's when she'd finally put her foot down and threatened to move into another bedroom if Matt didn't get treatment. He needed Viagra or something for erectile dysfunction. "Go see a doctor or leave me alone," she yelled, putting an end to what was beginning to feel like physical abuse.

Looking forlorn, Matt insisted his problem was stress related. A temporary situation.

Perhaps it was. Regina no longer cared. Having a limp penis humping hard against her vagina was a kind of torture she was no longer willing to endure.

At thirty-eight years old, Regina was at her sexual peak. She yearned to be aroused by extended foreplay. Her body ached for a substantially sized penis with girth and length that could produce heart-pounding, toe-curling orgasms.

Though she'd thought about cheating, seeking out a secret lover who could provide her with good sex was something she could not bring herself to do. Stuck in a passionless marriage, Regina sadly accepted that she and Matt would grow old together. And most likely, the location of her G-spot would remain an undiscovered mystery.

"Are you planning on upgrading Eric's phone?" Regina asked as she piled left-over spaghetti onto her husband's plate. To hell with waiting for Matt to bring up the subject.

Matthew Wheeler cocked his head and stared at the forkful of sauce-covered pasta. "What?"

"The new cell phone in the basement," she informed him. "It's for Eric, isn't it?"

"Oh!" He nodded enthusiastically and shoveled in the food. Between chews, he added, "Yeah, you know how he likes all the latest gadgets. He told me the phone we bought him back in September is already obsolete." Matt laughed heartily.

We? Regina gave Matt a disapproving look. "I fail to see any humor in this."

"What?" Matt asked with a shrug.

"Since you started your business, you're constantly complaining about money. We have to tighten up our spending—isn't that what you tell me? So why would you buy that boy a new phone just because he likes new gadgets? Didn't you give him money for clothes, a cell phone, and an expensive laptop at the beginning of the school year?"

Matt held up his hands in surrender. "You're right. I know I go overboard for Eric. But he's my only nephew…"

Regina glared at Matt.

"All right. I'll take the phone back tonight; there's a little strip mall with a T-Mobile store near one of my buildings. I just thought Eric would get a kick out of the new phone."

Regina shook her head. "He has a mother, you know. Why do you have to indulge his every whim? Can't your sister contribute anything for Eric?"

Matt's face hardened. The subject of his irrational commitment to his sister and her son was touchy, an off-limits topic that Regina rarely approached. But today she felt righteously indignant. She had to hide handbags bought with money she earned while Matt doted on someone else's child.

"Did I tell you Eric's going to be working with me this summer when he gets out of school?" Matt said cheerfully.

"No, you didn't mention it," Regina mumbled, lips pressed together in irritation. "What does that have to do with the new phone?"

"The new phone is on my plan. I can communicate with Eric at no extra charge. It'll really come in handy if he's working at one building while I'm at another. As soon as he learns the ropes, I plan to make him supervisor."

Regina rolled her eyes. "That boy's never done one day of hard labor. Eric needs to focus on getting into college, not learn the necessary skills to supervise a pack of conniving lowlifes. My God, Matt, he's just a teen-ager. He's not emotionally prepared for the drug-related antics of your work crew."

"What antics?" Matt asked, his voice rising. "What do you know about my employees?"

"I know that they're all drug addicts and alcoholics."

"My employees are all in recovery, Regina," Matt said defensively. "They're trying to get their lives together and they're doing a fine job."

"And their labor is cheap. That's the best part of the deal, isn't it?" she said sarcastically.

"What's the real problem, Regina? Are you upset because I'm spending so much time away from home or are you jealous because I latched onto something that has the potential to change our status in life—something I can leave Eric."

"I'm not jealous. I realize long hours are part of the process. As far as your nephew's concerned, maybe it's comforting for you to play 'pretend pop,' but it hurts me deeply that you hardly ever speak your own son's name." For a moment Regina was quiet. "Would it kill you to say Devon's name once in a while?"

"What's there to say? Devon's gone," Matt said bitterly. "What do you want me to say?"

"That you miss him," she said with a whimper.

Matt didn't answer. Regina leaned against the counter and stared at the kitchen floor.

Matt finished his meal in silence. Regina immediately turned around and began stacking dishes in the dishwasher. Their marriage was failing—had failed years ago. Were they headed for divorce court? Regina wanted to cry. Her husband's love for her was so sincere and they'd endured all the bumps in the road that life had thrown their way. But most important, he was faithful. Had always been. How many women could make that claim?

She loved her husband, but she no longer desired him sexually. She hated the sexual part of their relationship. And she despised the fact that he'd replaced their son so easily.

Matt cleared his throat. "I just remembered. I have to get an oil change before I pick up my crew. With all the miles I've been putting on the van, I don't want to take any chances and mess up my engine." He attempted to speak in a neutral tone, pretending there wasn't tension in the room.

He wiped his mouth with a napkin and stood, reached in his pocket, and peeled off three fifties. "Buy yourself something a new purse or something." Giving his wife a sad smile, he laid the money on the kitchen table.

It was his way of saying he was sorry about his seeming lack of regard for their son's memory. Regina nodded sadly and turned back to the dishwasher. Matt patted her back apologetically and threw down another fifty on his way out the door.

Regina went upstairs and put the money Matt had given her inside her Coach Patchwork Denim wallet. She'd add five hundred more and buy the Valentino braided tote that she'd been lusting for. Even the prospect of spending money on a prized possession that she wouldn't have to hide did nothing to elevate her mood.

Grappling with a barrage of negative thoughts, Regina sat on her bed, clutched a pillow to her bosom, and rocked. But the rocking motion did not soothe her. She felt agitated. So agitated she snatched the pillow away from her chest, folded it, and stuck it between her legs.

Squeezing the pillow with her thighs, she closed her eyes and imagined being plundered by a vulgar faceless man who was hung like a horse. He forced himself inside her, smacking her face when she pleaded for him to be gentle—to have mercy. It was a wickedly delicious fantasy that made her juices overflow and soak through the pillowcase.

During her fantasy, she used crude language, making sexual demands she'd never made with her husband. "Fuck me with that big dick. Split my pussy wide open," she shouted as her vaginal muscles contracted rapidly. "Goddamn!" she screamed as she exploded. Her face was twisted in a grimace, her heart pounding loudly and pumping so hard, it frightened her. Gasping for breath, Regina rubbed her chest in a circular motion. Finally, the spasms subsided and Regina was catapulted back to the reality of her own bedroom, lying in her marital bed with a pillow stuffed between her legs.

She let out a long sigh. Her life was so sad. Pitiable. Her husband was sexually disabled and refused to seek help. She was so deprived she'd resorted to fucking a damn pillow. Ashamed and feeling hopeless, she flung the pillow to the floor and quickly grabbed another, this time placing it on her face to muffle her sobs. She was certain that she loved her husband. After twenty years of marriage, he was like an extension of her, like an arm or leg, and she couldn't imagine life without him.

But she was dying inside. And it was Matt's fault. He didn't care that his limp dick had never given her an orgasm. He was perfectly content to continue their macabre sex dance. She'd talked about it and talked about it until she was blue in the face, but Matt was in denial. He said he was going through a phase—that he was anxious about his new business venture. Whatever! The fact remained that she was an unfulfilled woman who was locked in a sexless marriage.

Sleeping with another man for sexual satisfaction was out of the question. How could she ever look at herself in the mirror if she broke her marriage vows? And despite everything, she really loved Matt.

Regina exhaled. She'd just have to exercise more patience. In the meantime, she'd try to figure out a way to coerce Matt into getting professional help. He really needed to see a doctor. A sex therapist. An acupuncturist. Hell, she'd send him to a hypnotist. Perhaps the power of suggestion could help him keep his dick hard.

CHAPTER 2

Matthew Wheeler inspected the first four offices that Theo had cleaned. The trash bins were emptied with fresh liners tied around the rim, desk tops gleamed, and not a speck of debris dotted the carpets. Except for the telltale scent of alcohol that permeated the air, Theo had done a superb job. "Theo," Matt yelled over the noise of the vacuum cleaner down the hall.

Theo shut off the vacuum cleaner and stepped out into the hallway. "Whassup, boss?"

After working in a factory for damn near twenty years, being called "boss" was music to his ears. His heart instantly softened toward Theo. "Man, I can smell liquor in every office you cleaned."

"I ain't..."

Matt held up a hand. "Theo, you're supposed to be in recovery, man. The state pays me for the work you do. I could lose my contracts if somebody finds out you're drinking on the job. If you want to drink after work, that's your business." Matt narrowed his eyes. "If I smell liquor on you again"—he inhaled—"I'd hate to do it...but I'm going to have to let you go. "

"My bad. I'm gonna get it together. I needed a little taste to take the edge off."

"Take the edge off after I drop you off. All right, man?"

"Sure thing, boss. Thank you, Mr. Wheeler."

Matt smiled inside, but kept up a stern demeanor. "Now, go back over all the rooms you cleaned and spray some of that pine-scented deodorizer."

"I'm on it." Theo rushed to his cleaning cart, grabbed the spray, and began fumigating the four offices that held the lingering scent of cheap whiskey.

Matt walked past one of his other workers, Doug Faison, and gave the man a nod of approval. Mr. Faison, as everyone called him, was in his mid-fifties. He'd suffered two cocaine-related heart attacks. Not wanting to be responsible for the man's third heart attack, Matt gave him the easy task of lobby detail. All he had to do was empty and line a few trash bins, straighten out the magazines in the rack, dust and polish the mahogany desk, and wipe down the glass-topped end tables. No heavy labor for Mr. Faison.

The floor man, Langston Belgrave, was a big strapping man—built like a heavyweight fighter. Strong as an ox, he did the work of three men. It was said that the man had Indian blood. Matt didn't doubt it. A good-looking man with high cheekbones, a ruddy reddish-brown complexion, and bone-straight black hair that hung past his shoulders, Langston had the look of an authentic American Indian. Everyone called him "Cochise" and the name suited him perfectly.

Wearing earphones while bobbing his head in time to music only he could hear, Cochise lifted his chin in greeting when Matt approached. He moved rhythmically as he pushed the buffer across the shiny conference room floor. Cochise put in a hard day's work that more than made up for the slow-moving Mr. Faison's sluggish and uninspired cleaning.

Onika Brandt, the only female member of the crew, used slow motions as she cleaned the metal door frame of the sliding doors at the main entrance. With her back to Matt, she stretched a long sinewy arm as she wiped the metal ledge at the top of the doors. There was indifference in her movement as if her mind was on something more interesting than the cleaning task at hand.

Tall and wiry and without any curves, there was nothing glamorous about Onika. Her face was average. Her chin-length hair was worn in a simple wrap. More often than not, she pulled her hair back into a plain ponytail. But despite her uninteresting physical characteristics, Onika had sex appeal. And a lot of attitude. She was tough and sassy with a swagger in her walk that hinted at more than just a trace of wildness. Yes, Onika was tough, but she was soft and sugary where it counted.

Matt crept behind her, cozying up to her as he wrapped his arms around her tiny waistline and then inched his hands up to her breasts. Onika squealed in surprise as he cupped her nugget-sized breasts.

Spinning around, she said, "You scared the shit outta me." She swiftly pulled off the rubber gloves and wrapped her arms around Matt's neck. "You better stop sneaking up on me like that," she warned with a mischievous smile and then quickly brushed her lips against his.

Matt tried to prolong the kiss, but Onika pulled away. She wagged a finger at him. "I'm serious. Don't sneak up on me like that. You might give me a heart attack or a stroke or something."

"You're too young for that, baby." He gazed at her longingly. "Humph, if I keep messing around with you, I might end up stroking out."

Onika blushed. "Aw, you're not that old, Mr. Wheeler."

His eyes dimmed. "After all this time, you're still calling me Mr. Wheeler."

"You're not old, Matt," she corrected awkwardly. "You're just right."

"Prove it," he challenged.

"Is it break-time, yet?"

"It is for you. Put your cart away and meet me in the chairman's office in ten minutes."

Ten minutes later, Onika knocked. "It's open," Matt said softly as he swiveled in the dark-brown leather executive chair. The darkened room was softly illuminated by the glow from the brass desk lamp.

She walked around the desk and climbed on Matt's lap, straddling him. He raised her uniform and was delighted to find she wasn't wearing panties. He lifted her off his lap and placed her upon the enormous mahogany desk. She sat on the edge of the desk, facing him.

"Spread your legs, baby. Let Daddy get you in the mood."

Onika pulled her knees apart. She leaned back, her palms pressed against the smooth desktop. Her parted legs dangled over the polished mahogany wood. Still seated, Matt scooted forward and bent his head. He kissed one thin thigh and then the other, working his way up to her mound. He nipped at her pubic hairs, pulling them softly with his teeth. Matt knew Onika loved it when he pulled her pussy hairs. Her moans of appreciation excited him.

Trying to have sex with his wife was a monumental task. His dick didn't want to cooperate. Regina blamed him for his erection problems and wanted him to seek help. Matt gave a snort. All he had to do was sniff Onika's pussy and his dick stirred to life. One taste of her delicious nectar gave him a bulging erection.

Matt released her pubic hairs and pressed the tip of his tongue against her clit. He kept his tongue still, encouraging Onika to gyrate against it. When her juices began to trickle down his chin, he thrust his tongue between her folds, sucking and slurping until her moans escalated to a pitch that was entirely too loud. "Be quiet, baby," he cautioned.

"It's so good. I can't help it," Onika whined.

"You gotta be quiet," Matt whispered. "The fellas might come running up here thinking somebody's hurting you."

Onika giggled and pulled Matt's head back to her hot spot. But he stiffened his shoulders, resisting the urge to suck her sweet moisture.

Onika raised a brow. "Why'd you stop? I was just getting started."

Matt softly smacked her thigh and tugged at her arm. "Get up." He lifted her off the massive desk. "We're gonna switch places; I want you to sit on Daddy's face."

He loved referring to himself as "Daddy." Onika was only twenty years old and her youth made Matt feel good. Offering oral sex was something he'd never done with his wife. Eating pussy had never seemed appealing. But Onika kept his dick hard and he was happy to suck her clit. The girl's juices were like a sex drug. She was driving him crazy. Had his heart thumping with love.

Matt stretched his body across the desk. Onika climbed over his broad chest, lifted her dress, squatted over his face, and then lowered herself.

He pleasured her with his lips and his tongue. Her arms flailed; her fingers clenching and unclenching as she clawed at the air in an attempt to grab hold of something—anything. Finding nothing to grasp, she bent forward. Tilting her ass upward, she grabbed the edge of the desk and humped Matt's face.

Onika rubbed her pussy against his lips, his nose, and his forehead. Then she rotated her hips. Fast. Without restraint. Like she was an electric mixer and Matt's face was cake batter.

Her body tensed. She lifted up, but Matt pulled her back onto his face. "Smother me, baby," he whispered into her bushy mound.

"Yo, that's enough pussy eating. I'm ready for some dick."

"Just a little longer," he begged. Obliging him, Onika resumed squatting on his face, this time completely covering his nasal passage with her vagina.

"I can't breathe," Matt gasped. He thrashed as he struggled for air. Onika scooted up until her pussy brushed against his eyelids and her ass covered his nose. He tried to throw the slender woman off, but Onika maintained the position. "Baby, I can't breathe." His chest heaved as he tried to catch a breath of air.

Finally, she eased off his face. She looked at his groin and gave a self-satisfied smile.

"It's hard, baby. Daddy's ready for you," Matt said, gasping.

Onika slid off the desk and got down on the thick carpeted office floor. Lying spread eagle, she waited for Matt.

Instead of mounting her, Matt collapsed beside Onika. "You gotta get on top, baby. You wore your old man out."

"Stop saying that, Mr. Wheeler," she admonished with a giggle and then climbed on top of him. She aimed his stiffness into the center of her wet vagina. "Ain't nothing old about you," she whispered as she lowered herself onto his slippery but short pole. As soon as he penetrated, he ejaculated. He shuddered violently and emitted loud orgasmic moans, forgetting his request that he and Onika keep their voices low.

"Damn!" he murmured in disgust when he finally caught his breath. "I hate it when I cum quick. I told you I'm too old for you. You need a younger man. I can't do anything for you," he complained.

Comforting him, Onika put her arms around Matt and kissed his lips. "It's gonna get better, Mr. Wheeler. You lasted a lot longer this time."

"How much longer? A couple of seconds?" Matt sounded near tears. "You deserve better. Go on and get yourself a young man; somebody that can hang for hours."

"I don't want nobody else."

"Well, I'm not gonna mess with you anymore, Onika. I'm tired of embarrassing myself."

A knock on the door startled the pair. "Who is it?" Matt said gruffly.

"It's Theo. You want me to clean in there, Mr. Wheeler?"

"No, I got this one. Finish up the second floor."

"I'm finished. I was looking for Onika. She's supposed to wipe off all the telephones and clean the inside and outside of the cabinets on the second floor."

"She's on break," Matt bellowed. "Can't you cover for her?"

"No problem, boss," Theo said and hurried away from the chairman's office.

Lying on the floor, wrapped in each other's arms, Matt gave Onika a long, impassioned kiss. Breaking the kiss, he searched her face. "Are you sure you want me?"

"You know I do. Why do you keep asking me that? Don't I show you how I feel?"

"You sure do, baby," Matt said. "With my problem and all... well, I can't help wondering if I'm pleasing you as much as you're pleasing me."

"Mr. Wh..." She paused when Matt gave her a look. "I mean, Matt. I ain't never had nobody like you before. I'm not even worried about our little sex problem. We'll work it out."

"What about the fact that I'm a married man? Doesn't that bother you?"

Onika shook her head. "No, I can deal with it."

A relieved grin covered Matt's face. "Baby, you're too good to be true. Seriously, you're everything I ever wanted in a woman. I promise you, nothing is going to interfere with our relationship. Not my marriage—my business. Nothing. You're number one."

Onika beamed. "Aw, you're so sweet."

"I'm serious, baby. Every second of my spare time I have is gonna be spent with you." He cradled her chin. "You got me whipped. You know that, don't you?"

Blushing, Onika nodded.

"All right, let's get downstairs and act like we're working before Theo comes up here again."

Matt pulled Onika up. He kissed her again. "Oh yeah, look under the desk."

She furrowed her brow and bent to look under the desk. She picked up the T-Mobile bag and let out a delightful shriek when she uncovered the new cell phone.

"Thank you, Matt. You're so sweet." Onika covered Matt's hand with kisses.

"I'm tired of getting a busy signal every time I call you at the Recovery House. The phone is already charged and I put my cell phone number on lock; all you have to do is push a button to stay in touch."

"Matt," she said softly. "I know it's hard to believe, but I was out there messing with that stuff for so long; I never had much of nothing and I damn sure never had a cell phone that wasn't a throwaway or one I didn't steal off a sucka. I never had a legitimate hookup." She smiled at her gleaming new phone. "Thanks, Mr. Wheeler."

Being called Mr. Wheeler made Matt bristle, but he held his tongue and gave Onika a sympathetic pat on the shoulder. Poor Onika had started getting high when she was just sixteen and Matt hated that the young woman had experienced such hardship and seen so much ugliness in her short life. He intended to give her far more than just a cell phone. Onika was proving to be everything he desired in a woman. She deserved major props for being so patient with his erection and premature ejaculation problems.

He often kidded about being an old man, but in reality he felt he was too young to start taking Viagra. More than likely, his problem was psychosomatic. Having sex with the same woman for over twenty years had given him some serious dick problems.

However, with Onika in his life, Matt believed it would be just a matter of time before he was back on top of his game, stroking that thing and laying pipe for hours. Without a doubt, Onika was the antidote to his sex problems. And if he didn't watch himself, he was going to be completely strung out. Oh hell...who was he fooling? Onika had him whipped and he loved it.

CHAPTER 3

At the end of the evening, Matt and the male members of the crew loaded up the van with the heavy equipment. Carrying only her purse and a package of disposable cleaning cloths, Onika ambled to the back of the van and tossed in the package and then strolled over to the front passenger door. "Is it locked?" she yelled to Matt as she placed her hand on the door handle. Matt, still hard at work helping the fellows load up the van, responded by clicking a button to disarm the lock.

"Whassup, Onika? You too cute to help us out back here?" an irritated Cochise asked.

"Stop frontin', Cochise," she said, laughing. "You know I don't do no heavy lifting."

"Seems like you don't do much of nothing," Cochise complained, shooting Matt an accusatory look.

Matt ignored the look and gave an industrial-sized carpet cleaner a hard shove inside the van. With all the equipment accounted for and loaded, Matt slammed the door. "Let's go, fellows," he said, wiping his hands down the front of his shirt.

Eager to bring the work evening to a close and more than ready to get his drink on, Theo pulled open the side door and hopped in. Mr. Faison shuffled along behind him. With a toothpick jutting defiantly out the side of his mouth, Cochise gave Matt a dark, brooding look before he stepped inside the van.

Matt wondered if Cochise had caught on to his relationship with Onika. He wouldn't have been surprised. It wasn't as if he and Onika had been terribly discreet. Yeah, Cochise knew what was up and was probably miffed that while he worked like a mule, Onika barely lifted a finger, yet she made the same amount of money as he.

Matt had no intention of placating Cochise. One wouldn't expect such a big ole fellow to be so damn temperamental. It was probably that Apache blood or whatever the hell he was mixed up with that made the man so sullen at times. Matt figured that if Cochise didn't like the way he did business, he could take his recovering alcoholic, Indian-looking self and go work somewhere else. He wasn't doing Matt any favors. Unskilled labor came a dime a dozen. Cochise should be grateful.

Headed for Chester, Matt wheeled the van onto I-95 south. Mr. Faison fell asleep the moment the wheels started turning. Theo sipped liquor from a Pepsi bottle. Through the rearview mirror, Matt stole a glance at Cochise. Still wearing headphones, the man appeared to be glaring at the back of Onika's head as she fiddled with her new phone, trying out different ring tones.

Matt felt uneasy. To be honest, he couldn't afford to lose Cochise. Not just yet. His business was new and without Cochise's tireless labor, he'd never finish cleaning the three contracted buildings on time. He didn't want to lose any of his contracts; he wanted to gain more business. So, he supposed he'd better figure out a way to make Cochise happy. Yeah, he was going to have to stop showing favoritism and put Onika to work. She wasn't going to like it, but he'd make up for it.

After work, the crew got door-to-door service. The men lived at a group home on Seventh and Lloyd Streets in Chester and Onika lived at the women's home on Ninth and Lloyd. Matt dropped the men off first.

Alone at last with Onika, Matt took a detour and drove farther down Ninth Street and parked on a desolate spot behind Chester High School.

"I'm gonna get in trouble if I stay out here too late," Onika said. With a troubled look, she looked around the dark street.

"I can vouch for you, baby," Matt assured her. "I can say we had car trouble or something."

"Yeah, but will those nosey men back up your story?"

Matt ignored the question and started lifting her dress.

"Stop it, Matt. That shit ain't cool—not out here in the open."

"Just one taste, baby. That's all I want. Can Daddy get one taste before I make that lonely drive back to Philly?"

Onika smiled and shook her head. She pulled her dress up to her waist.

"Climb in the back and lie down."

Onika climbed to the backseat; Matt quickly joined her. She lay on her back with her knees up and pulled up her dress. Matt parted her knees and crouched between them, sniffing the crotch of the panties that she was now wearing. "I can smell your pussy, baby," he said, his voice muffled.

Onika cupped his face and held it firmly to her crotch. "What does it smell like?" she asked in a sultry whisper.

Matt took a deep sniff. "It smells nice and musky, baby—like pussy juice that's been marinating for hours." Matt surprised himself with his dirty talk. He never used such graphic language with his wife, but Onika brought out the freak in him.

"Taste it," Onika offered, pulling her panties to the side.

Stretching his tongue until it ached, Matt tried to stick it as deeply as possible. He slurped greedily. Onika quickly pushed his head away. "One taste, Mr. Wheeler, remember? I have to get home before I get in trouble."

"Stop calling me that," Matt said angrily as he reluctantly pulled his hungry lips away from Onika's tasty love hole.

"I'm sorry, but it's hard to remember what to call you. On the job, I'm supposed to call you Mr. Wheeler and when we're alone you want me to call you, Matt. It's confusing having to keep going back and forth like that."

"I'm sorry, Onika. It's not you, baby. It's our situation. You're a grown woman and yet you have a curfew like you're somebody's child. This group home situation is not going to work." Matt looked off in thought.

Onika checked out the time on her new cell phone. "Mr. Wheeler, I really have to go. If I break curfew and get kicked out, then what?" she asked, her eyes fixed on his.

Matt shook his head. "You don't get high anymore, do you?"

Onika grimaced. "No!"

"When's the last time you got high?"

She gave a throaty groan. "I told you—six months ago."

"Can you stay clean on your own? Do you really need that program?"

Onika shrugged. "I don't know if I'm strong enough to stay clean on my own."

"Well, what exactly are those people doing for you besides putting a roof over your head? And a dilapidated roof at that!"

"They make sure I get medical care, they got me the job with you so I can fit back into society, they make sure I attend my group meetings, and—"

"I can handle all that. Look, to hell with that group home. I'm gonna get you your own place. How does that sound?"

Onika gave a nervous smile. "It sounds like a dream, but I'm not gonna front, Mr. Wheeler, I'm scared to be on my own."

Matt turned sincere eyes toward Onika. "I'll help you. I'll make sure you have everything you need—physically, emotionally, and financially. There won't be any reason for you to get high."

Onika gave Matt a tight and distant smile. "My counselor said I'm going to have to attend meetings for the rest of my life."

"Your counselor must be crazy. Those people just want to have control over you. Look at all the rules they make you abide by, and the way they keep tabs on your coming and going. Seems like you're in some type of cult, if you ask me."

Onika laughed. "I gotta go." Slender enough to squeeze through the space between the driver's seat and passenger's seat, Onika climbed to the front of the van. Matt, however, got out of the van, opened the front door, and returned to the driver's seat.

He started the engine. "We gotta find some time to look for a place." He squinted in thought and then flashed her an encouraging smile. "We have to work Saturday…how about Sunday?"

Onika shifted uncomfortably. "Sounds good," she said flatly.

When Matt pulled up in front of the group home, he reached over to give Onika a kiss. She weaved away from him. "Chill, Mr. Wheeler. That nosey-ass house manager is probably peeking out the window. And until I'm situated in my own place I'm not taking any chances."

Disappointed, Matt restrained himself, puckered his lips, and gave Onika an air kiss.

"See you tomorrow night, Mr. Wheeler."

Matt watched her walk up the steps that led to the front door. He kept his eyes locked on her until the door opened and she was no longer in view. As he pulled off, he steered with one hand and used the other to unzip his pants. Stimulated by the musty smell on his upper lip and the acrid taste on his tongue, Matt stroked his meat throughout the entire drive home.

CHAPTER 4

Huddled under the bedspread and pretending to be asleep, Regina lay very still when she heard Matt climbing the stairs. She cringed at the thought of him pulling back the covers with the intention of selfishly awakening her for his own sexual gratification. *If he touches me, I'm going to scream*, she thought.

"Are you asleep?"

Lazily, she shifted her position, pretending he had awakened her. "Huh? What time is it?" She squinted at the clock. It was two-thirty in the morning. "You're home late."

"When you're working for yourself, you can't leave until the job's finished," Matt said defensively as he undressed.

Regina sat up. "I wasn't being accusatory, Matt. I was just making a statement."

"I'm sorry, baby. I guess I'm a little on edge because one of my people didn't show up," he lied. "And making matters worse, my nineteen-hundred-dollar automatic scrubber broke down on me… it just wasn't my night," he added to strengthen his case. "It's not easy being a black man trying to run a business."

Regina nodded at her husband sympathetically.

"Baby, I'm tired to the bone," he said, heading for the shower. When he returned to the bedroom, he pulled back the covers and got in the bed.

Luckily for Regina, Matt was sound asleep and snoring within minutes.

Wide awake, Regina stared into space. The combination of Matt's thunderous snoring and her racing thoughts kept her from going to sleep. How long could she go on like this? How long should she pretend that her sexuality was inconsequential? At her age, a woman was at the peak of her sensuality, yet Regina felt dead inside. Or was she? She thought about the pillow incident earlier that day. She shook her head in shame. She'd relieved her sexual tension with a damn pillow. Now, that was truly pitiful.

Then she thought about her sex life with Matt. The word that described what he did was *masturbation*. She suddenly realized that her husband, unable to maintain an erection and penetrate normally, had been masturbating on her for years.

Feeling violated and angry, Regina yanked the pillow from beneath Matt's head. In a deep sleep, he didn't stir. She folded it, placed it between her thighs, and turned over on her stomach. She conjured an image of the hard, big dick she needed and humped the pillow, but it wasn't working. Frustrated, she flung the pillow over at her sleeping husband. It landed on his face, but didn't mute his annoying snores.

Determinedly, she marched downstairs. She searched the fridge and found a perfectly sized cucumber. It was a bit chilly for her intended purpose, so Regina stuck it in the microwave for a couple of seconds and then wrapped it in a sandwich bag. She traipsed up the stairs carrying her homemade dick-in-a-bag.

In the bedroom, she slathered on lubricant, lay next to her comatose husband, and inched in the cucumber. The cucumber provided the girth her finger didn't possess, the hardness that a pillow couldn't give, and the stamina her husband had never had.

The volume of the orgasmic groan that escaped her throat surprised her. The internal earthquake that sent shudders throughout her body seemed to cause the bed to shake. It occurred to her that her orgasmic activity might awaken Matt, but she was too caught up in the throes of ecstasy to seriously give a damn.

Regina emitted one last moan as the violent orgasm subsided. Satiated, a wave of sleepiness began to close her eyes. Too tired to properly dispense of the cucumber, she pulled it out and let it roll beneath the covers.

A sweet and peaceful sleep soon claimed her.

CHAPTER 5

Regina and Matt ate their evening meal in silence. Regina hadn't created the tension. Due to her self-administered sexual release, her mood was bubbly and playful. Matt, on the other hand, seemed down in the dumps.

She wondered if he'd rolled out of bed that morning and had found the cucumber twisted up in the sheets. She stifled a giggle. It would be a hell of a wake-up call for a man to discover his wife had to resort to fucking a cucumber and it served him right if he did discover his phallus-like replacement. Maybe Matt would go get some medical help if caught a glimpse of his competition.

"What's wrong, honey? You're barely touching your food. Aren't you hungry?" she inquired.

Matt picked at his food and kept looking out the kitchen window. "I'm worried that it's going to rain. I'm screwed if it rains," he complained.

"Did you check the Weather Channel?"

"No, I don't have to; I can tell," he said grumpily. "Black folks don't want to work when it rains. I guarantee you, when I pull up at Ninth and Central, I'll be lucky if two workers show up. If the program was willing to pay for a couple more men I wouldn't have to constantly worry about the guys showing up when the weather's bad."

"The guys? Don't you have any women working in the program? It seems discriminatory to employ men only."

"Sure, I have one female worker, but to be honest, she's just a token. She can't really handle the equipment or perform the heavy labor. If I employed more women, I'd never get anything done."

"That's odd. At my job, our cleaning crew includes women and they handle the same equipment as the men. Anything too heavy to lift is picked up with a dolly. Anyone can do that. I think you need to reconsider your position on hiring women."

"If you're looking for an argument about my hiring practices, you can forget about it," Matt said harshly. "What you observe at the bank can't compare to being in the trenches with my employees—ex-addicts and alcoholics. People who have to be coddled like babies. Trying to get a good day's labor out of those rejects is like trying to supervise a bunch of schoolkids. One of my best and strongest men is always bitchin' because he thinks that my female worker should be pulling down the same amount of work as he does. Now, that's downright ridiculous."

"Well, Matt...you have to look on the bright side. The government's paying you to train these people and you're getting free labor. It's a win-win situation any way you look at it," Regina pointed out.

Matt was silent. Discontent surrounded him like a dark cloud.

Seeing that her husband didn't want to have his mood brightened, she left him alone and went into the living room. She clicked on the TV and scrolled down to the Weather Channel. "It's cloudy with a chance of a few light showers, Matt," Regina called out to her husband. "No torrential rain, so I imagine you'll be okay."

"I don't go by those forecasters," Matt said as he entered the living room. "Look, in case I end up having to put in some extra work, I'd like to get an early start. I'll see you tonight, baby." He gave Regina a quick peck on the cheek and was out the door.

Good riddance! Could life get any better? Another day of mercy had been bestowed upon her. No limp dick creating slimy friction against her thigh. She clicked off the TV and went into Matt's office and turned on the computer. She put in a Google search for sex toys for women and the first thing on the list was: Masturbation Toys for Women—Vibrators!

Excited, she clicked on the link and found herself scanning a delightful array of vibrators. The one that caught her attention was called The Jack Rabbit and featured a pearl pack designed to rotate inside your vagina while the pointed rabbit extension eagerly nibbled your clit. It sounded like exactly what the doctor ordered. No more pillows or cucumbers for her. She excitedly clicked a button, input her credit card number, and paid extra for one-day FedEx delivery. Dreamily, she imagined the convulsive orgasms she'd be experiencing soon.

CHAPTER 6

The group meeting had gone into overtime. Seemed like everybody felt like spilling their guts today. Being a good listener, Cochise, who was running the meeting, didn't rush anyone along. He let the men talk about their lives and what led to their addictions for as long as they needed. As for himself, he was a man of few words.

Although Cochise had told his story numerous times, he'd provided only sketchy details about his past. His past was nobody's business. The most he was willing to admit was that he'd been so devastated by a personal loss that he'd sought solace in a bottle of gin. Self-medicating morning, noon, and night, he drank until he was numb and unable to feel the pain. One day he woke up in a hospital bed, intravenous tubes running everywhere. He was diagnosed with alcohol poisoning and was lucky to be alive. Alcohol ruined his life. He'd lost everything, but he never took another drink. Now he was determined to rebuild. Being gainfully employed was just the beginning.

Cochise had big plans. The way he saw it, the dozens of men and women who lived at the Recovery House, a program with two locations—one for men and the other for women, needed life skills training as well as job training if they were ever going to become productive members of society. His plan was to write a proposal to get funding for a program that would help the hard-to-employ, recovering addicts get education and employment training. They needed the security of having real jobs with benefits. Bullshitting around with Mr. Wheeler provided a little chump change, nothing more.

Cochise had been clean for a year now and held the position of assistant house manager, which entitled him to his own room in the group home. It was a small room with a bed and a few crates to store his belongings, but it was his own private quarters and he was grateful. With the meeting now over, he returned to his room to get ready.

Packing his satchel, he threw in bottled water and a bandana to keep dust from his hair. He packed his iPod, his only purchase since he'd been working, and stuck some toothpicks in his shirt pocket. Chewing on toothpicks had become a habit, but at least it was a harmless one.

He checked the time. It was getting late; no time to do his regimented one hundred pushups. In fact, he'd have to jog to Shawna's apartment and hit it real quick if he expected to get to the pick-up spot on time.

Shawna was real cool. A friend with benefits. He'd met her on the subway. She was loaded down with bags and, being a gentleman, Cochise helped her carry some of her packages. They clicked right off the bat. There was an instant physical attraction, but Cochise had made it clear from jump that he wasn't looking for a committed relationship. Shawna co-signed, telling him that she'd had her heart broken so many times, the last thing she was looking for was another complicated relationship. A sex buddy was all she wanted, she assured him.

Sounded like a plan to Cochise, but before he got involved he had to be honest. "I'm a recovering alcoholic," he told Shawna. She nodded in understanding. "I have a ten o'clock curfew on weekends," he added and waited for a response. Shawna gave a nod. "And on weekdays," Cochise told her with a sigh, "I work from four to nine up in Philly. By the time I get back to Chester, it's pretty late and I have to check in at the Recovery House." He looked her in the eyes. "I'm not going try to hold you. My time is pretty much limited," he said apologetically.

"I can deal with it," Shawna said, which surprised the hell out of Cochise. "Holla when you can."

Cochise grinned from ear to ear. Damn, he had lucked up big time. But it was too soon to get excited. He hadn't told her about his dick. He didn't have anything to be ashamed of, but Cochise felt it was only fair to warn a potential sex partner that he had thirteen inches of length and his jawn was thick as shit. He had yet to meet a woman who could handle him until he took the time to open her up and stretch her walls out. Yeah, his dick was husky like a mufucka. He could injure a female real bad if he tried to push all his inches up in her. It took a while to open a female up. Cochise had to dole out the dick a little bit at a time, giving up just a few inches per sex session.

Shawna emitted moans of desire when he revealed that he was working with thirteen thick-ass inches. However, a few days later, when Cochise was ready to hit it and tried to ease just the head of his dick into her tight opening, she cried out in pain. "It hurts. Stop! It's too big. I can't do it!"

"Calm down, ma. I'm just gonna give a little bit of the head, aiight?"

Shawna nodded uncertainly.

When Cochise started stirring up her juices with his rounded cap, Shawna relaxed. Trying to be brave, she parted her legs a little wider. Cochise was tempted to force the entire bulbous head of his dick inside her moisture, but exercising self control, he kept his word and inserted just a portion of the rounded tip.

After a few moments, Cochise withdrew from her too-tight opening. He slathered lubricant on Shawna's soft, warm inner thighs, and guided himself into a space between them. As his long appendage glided in and out of Shawna's moisture-slick flesh, the shaft stroked her pussy lips and the huge, mushroom-capped head caressed her clit.

With his dick cushioned between her thighs, Cochise worked up a pulsating rhythm and Shawna matched every driving thrust. Ready to explode but not wanting to leave his partner unfulfilled, Cochise stopped pumping. He sat up and gently spread her female lips. "Mmm!" The sound came out in a throaty growl. The pussy was hot and juicy, looked like it was begging for some dick. Maybe Shawna could handle a couple inches. Looking at her soft pinkness made him bite his lip to suppress a loud groan. His pulsing dick had him so disoriented, he grabbed his manhood and started aiming for the source of warmth, momentarily unconcerned about inflicting pain or causing bodily harm.

"No," Shawna yelled, jolting Cochise to his senses. Looking frightened, she bolted up. "I can't do it. I can't take all that dick!"

He looked at the monstrous dick in his hand and released it. "I'm sorry. I know you can't handle all this," Cochise said soothingly. "I promise I won't hurt you," he assured her. "I just want to make you feel good. Aiight, ma? Trust me. Aiight?" His voice held a pleading tone.

Warily, Shawna eased back. Her legs were tense and trembled

in fear. Cochise kissed her neck, softly grazed each nipple with his teeth, and then moved downward, his long hair sweeping Shawna's torso, giving her an intense tingling sensation as if a dozen feathers caressed her body. Urging Shawna to trust him, Cochise kissed her pussy and then separated her labia even wider than before, as if preparing her tunnel for deep penetration. She shuddered and murmured sounds that were a mixture of fear and anticipation. "Relax, ma," he whispered, his breath warming the pink flesh of her opened pussy, causing it to contract with desire.

Cochise slid his shaft against her moist opening and massaged her swollen clit with the colossal helmet of his dick, giving Shawna dual pleasure.

Motivated by pleasure, Shawna threw her legs tightly around Cochise's back, pulling him closer, gaining better access to the tantalizing friction. Losing possession of her rational mind, she screamed, "Give it to me hard!" Shawna wasn't thinking clearly. Hot pussy had a way of making a woman talk shit she couldn't back up. Cochise, now in control of his libido, knew better than to give in to Shawna's desire. Without having her pussy walls sufficiently stretched, he knew she could end up in the emergency room with internal bleeding or badly damaged female organs.

Cochise allowed himself to be pulled in by Shawna's insistent thighs, but he refused to penetrate. Maintaining self-control, he stroked her parted pussy until he created friction that was so intense, Shawna moaned and clawed at his muscular shoulders and then raked her nails across his well-developed back. Her body trembled. Her creamy nectar coated the head of his dick and then trickled down his shaft.

"Please," she murmured, needing sexual release so badly she was willing to endure the pain of penetration from his mighty weapon. Unwilling to risk fucking up her insides, he licked the pussy until her body quaked. After Shawna's heart rate slowed down, she sat up, intending to return the favor. She guided Cochise's thickness to her mouth. He entered the warm, moist place slowly, rubbing the cap of his dick against the soft insides of her cheeks. With her tongue, she circled the portion of his length that fit inside her mouth and put a suction hold around his girth.

Her lips puckered around his rigid flesh. Though she could take in only a little more than a quarter of his length, her mouth worked on his hard meat, slurping and contracting like a vagina. Cochise wished he could push his dick all the way in. He'd never experienced the sensation of having his entire dick inside a woman's mouth. He took rapid breaths, imagining Shawna's lips wrapped around the base, his nuts brushing against her chin. The mental picture excited him, made his dick thump in preparation of jetting out a rush of cum. It would have been polite to ask if she swallowed, but Cochise was too far gone to think about good manners. Groaning, he ejaculated inside her warm mouth. It felt so good, he had to restrain himself from verbally thanking her. Speaking those words would have been corny as hell, so he let his loud moan convey his gratitude when he received the added pleasure of feeling her constricting throat as she swallowed his gushing load.

For a while, Shawna accepted their no-strings-attached sexual encounters, assuring Cochise that commitment was the last thing on her mind. But that was a few months ago. Today, judging by the look on Shawna's face after they'd had sex, the situation had clearly changed.

"Are you leaving already?" Shawna sounded disgruntled as she lay naked, curled on her side.

"Yeah. You know I have to go to work," he responded casually though he could tell Shawna was getting heated. While he stepped into his jeans, Shawna watched, her eyes filled with a combination of hurt and fury. Her shoulders rose as she inhaled anger and then sagged as she gave a long, sad sigh. "What's wrong?" he asked, though he knew the answer. It was obvious Shawna had caught feelings for him. Cochise was running late; he didn't have time to pacify her, to gently remind her that they'd both agreed to a friendship and not a love affair. He had to hustle out of her crib if he expected to meet the van on time. He knew Mr. Wheeler wouldn't leave him behind, but Cochise didn't feel like hearing the man give a speech about the virtues of being organized, the virtues of being prompt, the virtues of hard labor, and yada, yada, yada. Mr. Wheeler had a lot of nerve complaining about anything with the way he was carrying on with Onika. What a hypocrite. A married man getting it on with a young girl half his age.

Shawna sniffled, demanding Cochise's attention.

"Yo, what's wrong?" he asked again.

"*You're* what's wrong, Cochise. How do you think I feel, watching you jump into your clothes two seconds after you bust a nut?"

"I gotta go to work, ma. Why you trying to have beef with me like I'm doing something wrong?" Cochise gathered his blanket of dark hair and pulled it back into a neat ponytail.

She poked out her lips. "How come you never do anything nice—like bring me flowers or take me out to dinner?"

"Yo, we cool and everything, but you know it's not like that. I thought we were on the same page."

Shawna looked at him askance. "Give me the page number. Since I can't even get a real kiss me or any type of affection, I know I'm on the wrong page. Shit, I doubt if we're even on the same chapter. You treat me like I'm some type of sex toy—a blow-up doll—or pocket pussy," Shawna complained, showing a feisty side Cochise had never seen.

Cochise checked his watch. He had to roll out. "Look, I thought we had an arrangement. I guess I was wrong. Maybe we should stop seeing each other." His words came out sounding cruel, so he tried to soften them. "I'm not trying to hurt you, Shawna. I'm not cold-hearted like some dudes, but I told you what it is from the door." Cochise refused to let Shawna guilt him into something he wasn't ready for.

"Oh! It's like that? The minute I speak my mind, you want to put the brakes on our relationship. I can't believe you want to end it, just like that!" Shawna snapped her fingers for emphasis. "You have a lot of nerve treating me like crap after all I've done for you."

Cochise frowned. "We gave each other pleasure. I didn't take anything I didn't give."

"Oh no? Well, your dick's not bent out of shape, is it?"

Cochise frowned, not comprehending.

"Yeah, your dick hasn't changed at all, but my pussy is all beat up. You're walking out the same way you came in but I'm left with damaged goods. I should've stuck with letting you bust a nut between my thighs. I must have been crazy to let you put your big-ass dick all the way up in my pussy, stretching it out so wide, a regular-sized man won't be able to feel shit when he's up in it. He's gonna feel like he just dropped his dick inside the Grand fucking Canyon! Who do you think is going to want to have sex with a gutted-out, deformed pussy? When a nigga pushes up in a bitch, he wants to feel some tight walls clenching up around his shit."

The degree of Shawna's anger was disturbing. Cochise felt guilty. He walked over to the bed and rubbed Shawna's shoulder. She misunderstood the gesture. Thinking he'd had a change of heart, Shawna reached for his other hand, kissing his fingers and the back of his hand with fervent devotion.

Gently, Cochise withdrew his hand. "I just wanted to tell you," he said awkwardly, "um, your vagina will shrink back over time. It'll shrink down to the size of the next man—"

Shawna flinched as if his words had scorched her ears. "Fuck you, Cochise," she exploded. "Get out!"

CHAPTER 7

B*lackouts* was the name given to new admissions who were fresh off the hellish streets and who were still lethargic from detoxing. The haggard-looking and poorly attired women looked at Onika and her fancy cell phone with the yearning of morbidly obese young girls watching Rihanna prance half-naked across the television screen.

"I'm out," Onika yelled to the house manager, who was in the kitchen overseeing the preparation of the evening meal.

"You got your key?" the woman bellowed from the kitchen.

"Yup," she said, jiggling her keys. "See you when I get off from work tonight." Before bouncing out the door, Onika turned to the dull-eyed *blackouts* and gave them a triumphant smile, informing them that her world was much better than theirs.

Mr. Faison and Theo were already sitting in the van when Onika arrived at the corner of Ninth and Central. She eased into the front seat, her unspoken designated spot. "Where's Cochise?" she asked, turning to the two men in the back. They responded with mumbles and shrugs. She gave Matt a questioning look.

"I don't know what's up with Cochise and his moody self," Matt said. "But if he wants to stay in this program…"

Strolling toward the van, shoulders hunched, hands stuffed in his pockets, brows furrowed, Cochise looked mad at the world.

Without an apology or explanation for his lateness, he got into the van and maneuvered his large frame into the seat behind Theo and Mr. Faison. His facial expression forbade anyone to question him.

And no one did. There was a collective sigh of relief among the three workers. Cochise's arrival assured them of a lighter work load.

Matt was relieved as well, but didn't let it show. He demonstrated his disapproval of Cochise's tardiness by making a wide and screeching U-turn into oncoming traffic. Onika let out a cry and grabbed the overhead handle while Mr. Faison fell across Theo's lap. Theo pushed the man off and took a quick nip from his flask.

"Yo, man. You don't have to try to kill us to get your point across," grumbled Cochise. "I'm five minutes late, so sue me." Cochise snapped on his headphones, closed his eyes, and ignored everyone for the duration of the ride to Philly.

On Fridays, Matt and the crew cleaned a building on Germantown Avenue, a building where a host of black professionals rented space. There was a black law firm, an accounting firm, an optician, a dental practice, and a chiropractor. Matt hated the place. There was always some stuffed shirt, some pompous-ass Negro roaming the premises, following Matt and his crew, pointing out what required special attention. On one occasion, the chiropractor, a wizened old kook who didn't look like he had the strength to crack anyone's bones, sauntered up to Matt and pointed out a smudge on the doorknob to his office. Matt couldn't imagine how a busy professional had the time to inspect a damn doorknob. Now, his white clientele...they left him alone, allowed his crew to work in peace. If they had complaints, they put it in writing.

For Matt, however, the worst part of cleaning that building on Germantown Avenue was that he had no private time with Onika. And being alone with Onika had quickly become his top priority.

Matt swung up to the building. "Listen up, fellas. I have a new contract up in the Tioga section. It's light work, so I shouldn't be more than an hour or so. You guys know the routine…start with the dental office and work your way up," Matt instructed. "Onika's gonna take the ride with me and handle the dusting and polishing and whatnot."

Onika frowned. "What? Why do I have to go with you?" She stretched her neck anxiously to the back of the van. "Take Mr. Faison," she urged.

"No, I need him to handle the lobby," Matt said.

Cochise usually put up a fuss about the unfairness of Onika getting all the easy assignments. But not today. He and the other two workers seemed resigned to the favoritism that was bestowed upon her. Cochise bobbed his head to the music, giving no sign of his usual righteous indignation.

After the guys unloaded the equipment, Matt swung the van into traffic and headed for North Philly. Onika rode in hostile silence. He parked in front of a cheap hotel on the corner of Broad and Poplar that rented rooms by the hour. Onika was quite familiar with the hotel; it had been one of her haunts back when she was hustling for rock, but goddamn, she was in recovery now. Didn't she deserve a come-up? Would it kill the cheap bastard to get a room in a real hotel?

She recognized the clerk at the front desk and he recognized her. He gave Onika a wink as he handed Matt the key to room 207.

The musty-smelling shit hole of a room brought back memories—exciting memories that put goose bumps up and down her arms as she recalled the euphoric feeling of being high. Suddenly, Onika felt antsy; there was no way in hell she could put up with Mr. Wheeler's bad fucking without some assistance. A couple of hits off the pipe shouldn't hurt.

"I'll be right back; I have to go to the bathroom," she said anxiously as she exited the room under the pretense of going to the restroom at the end of the hall. She detoured down the stairs and rapidly headed for the front desk. Batting her lashes at the clerk, she leaned across the desk. "Whassup, Duke?"

"Whatcha need?" Duke asked.

Onika held up two fingers.

In exchange for two balled-up ten-dollar bills, Duke stealthily handed Onika a piece of white rock wrapped in a torn corner of a sandwich bag that was tied at the end—a makeshift crack container.

"You gotta pipe?"

Duke stared at her in disgust. "Where's your shit?"

"I've been clean for a minute."

"I ain't got no pipe for you to borrow, but I'll sell you a kit for ten bucks." He reached under the desk and brought up a cylindrical glass tube and a mesh screen.

Frowning, Onika examined the pipe. "That cheap shit will probably bust the minute I put some heat on it."

"Whatever," Duke said, "You can walk around the corner to the store if you think you can get something better, but I can guarantee you, they gonna sell you the same shit. You know the deal, Onika. How they gonna get return customers if they sell sturdy-ass, unbreakable pipes? You gotta work with what you got."

"That's fucked up," she said, tossing Duke an additional ten dollars before trotting off to the bathroom.

Fifteen minutes later, she was back in room 207. She scowled as she examined her fingertips, which were charred from repeatedly flicking the flame to the pipe.

"What happened? I was starting to worry about you," Matt said, looking flustered.

"I'm straight." But Onika sounded far from straight. Her words were slightly garbled, like she didn't quite know where to place her tongue.

Horny as hell, Matt didn't notice. Naked and lying prone, he beckoned her. "Come on, baby, we ain't got a lot of time. Sit on my face real quick so my dick can get hard."

Feeling high enough to be able to put up with her limp-dick sugar daddy, Onika glided over to the bed, pulled off her panties, and straddled Matt's face.

Matt flicked his tongue against Onika's clit and then gently trapped it between his teeth, tongue lashing it until Onika moaned. The sexy sounds that escaped her lips prompted Matt to jut his tongue into her opening. His tongue caressed her vaginal walls, licked places inside her pussy hole that his small penis could never reach. Using his tongue the way he wished he could use his dick, Matt jutted it in and out at a frenzied pace.

"Fuck me, Mr. Wheeler; I need your big dick up in me." Onika spoke the words without emotion, like a poorly trained actress in a porn flick.

Matt knew his appendage was far from being big, but he loved that Onika found it to be so. "Here I come, baby," he exclaimed, turning Onika on her back and spreading her legs. "I'm gonna give you all this big dick!" He started groaning and spurting cum before he even touched her vagina.

Making the best of his quick ejaculation, Onika got up and raced to the bathroom to get a couple more hits. "Gotta go wash up; be right back."

"Hey, baby, what's that smell?" Matt asked when she returned a few minutes later.

Onika shrugged. "What smell?"

"I don't know." He sniffed at the air. "Like a burning cigarette, but stronger."

Fury distorted her facial features. "How the hell am I supposed to know what goes on in this shit hole?" Glaring at him, she folded her arms in irritation. "Can you let me hold something?"

"How much?" he asked warily.

"A couple beans."

"You know I don't speak that ghetto language, Onika. How much are you asking for?"

"Two or three hundred dollars, or as much as you can give me."

"What for? You know I planned to put a down payment on that apartment Saturday, and you're going to need furniture. Baby, I'm not rich; we're going to have to tighten up a little."

"I need my hair done," she said huffily. She frowned down at her nails. "All this cleaning and polishing I do on the job is fucking with my fingernails. I need a manicure, too."

Against his better judgment, but unable to refuse her request, Matt dug into his pocket and brought out a twenty and a ten. "Baby, this is all I have on me right now. You can get your nails done with this, can't you?"

She sucked her teeth. "What about my hair?" she asked sulkily and then snatched the bills from his hand.

"I'll have more cash tomorrow." Matt sounded grieved.

"How much?" Onika perked up.

"I'll try to get my hands on an extra hundred."

"That's all?" Onika poked out her lips.

"Or two," Matt added. "Baby, please get back in bed. You've got me in the mood again. You look so sexy when you're angry with me."

Onika rolled her eyes to show him just how angry she was. "I have to pee."

"Again?"

"Yeah," she responded with defiance. "Do you think I like walking all the way down the damn hall to take a piss?"

Matt watched in silence as Onika sashayed out of the room. Two minutes later, she made another purchase from Duke and this time she stayed in the bathroom for twenty minutes.

Onika came back to the room wearing a more pleasant expression than when she'd left. Taking advantage of her improved mood, Matt made a bold request. "Get on your hands and knees for me, baby."

His words drew a look of disbelief from Onika. "Why? You wanna try to hit it doggy-style?" As high as she was, she knew there was no way his little dick could accomplish that feat.

"No, I want to do something else," he said eagerly, breathing hard as he assisted in positioning her on all fours. He pried her legs apart, creating a lot of space between them. Then he crawled up behind her and began slowly licking her pussy from behind. Onika pushed her tiny ass up in the air to accommodate the pussy-licker, giving him plenty of access to her love hole. She could feel frenetic movement behind her and knew he was jerking himself off, which was fine with her.

His tongue, in sync with his hand, worked at a feverish pace. He licked her pussy so fast and so deep, Onika seemed to vibrate until she released a glob of sticky honey. Matt lapped up every drop; he even sucked off the stickiness that was embedded in her pubic hairs. Making a young girl climax boosted Matt's ego. He raised his head, beaming with pride.

"You're a freak, Mr. Wheeler," Onika approved with a lazy grin.

Back in his room after work later that night, Cochise, trying to forget the pained look in Shawna's eyes, the hysteria in her voice, decided to work on his proposal. He wished he had access to a computer, but since he didn't the proposal was handwritten. In a black and white composition book, Cochise had outlined a proposal to apply for a grant to train and provide gainful employment for recovering addicts, ex-cons, the outcasts from society who most often returned to unhealthy lifestyles due to their inability to earn a decent living.

Cochise opened the top dresser drawer and groped around for a pen. As he rummaged through the drawer, his fingers touched upon a sharp edge. Curious, he pulled it out and instantly wished he hadn't. It was a cheap metal picture frame. Instead of a glass covering, a dented dusty plastic square protected the photograph.

At first he smiled sadly at the photograph. The painful memory slowly crept into his mind and then struck like a blow that made Cochise grunt in agony and stumble backward until his large, muscular body fell upon the creaky narrow bed. Rocking and moaning, Cochise cried out her name. *Tierra*. God help him… the pain was intense. He needed a drink.

Raising up slightly, he looked around his barren room, his arm outstretched as if it were possible that a bottle of gin might miraculously materialize in his hour of need. He thought of taking his few dollars and hitting the nearest bar. But he endured the emotional turmoil until it passed and clear thinking returned.

Instead of replacing the picture in the dresser drawer, Cochise carefully wrapped the photograph in a pillowcase and placed it on the top shelf of the closet. He pushed it into a far corner behind a pile of old T-shirts, seldom-worn sweaters, and other old clothing, where he wouldn't likely come across Tierra's picture anytime soon.

CHAPTER 8

Regina felt light-hearted and a little guilty, as if she was cheating on Matt with her new package. The vibrating penis with the clit-nibbling attachment had her all aglow and in a state of calm that was an entirely new sensation.

Poor Matt had been replaced by an inanimate object, she mused sadly. Then, mentally shifting gears, she angrily reminded herself of the years of sexual frustration and how Matt seemed content to allow her to spend the rest of her life without ever experiencing an orgasm. He was so selfish. And she was also to blame. Seeking gratification from compulsive spending on unnecessary purchases was sick. She should have seen a shrink years ago. Surely a psychiatrist would have used some psychobabble to point out that Regina's handbag fetish was a cry for a stiff dick.

Matt was still asleep. Knowing he was probably worn out from working his two jobs all week, she didn't want to disturb him and began dressing as quickly and quietly as possible.

On Saturdays Regina and Matt usually went out to eat or they stayed at home and ate something that was easy to prepare, but after another bout with her new sex toy, she felt hungry and was in a good enough mood to want to cook a good meal for her husband.

The moment she slipped on a pair of pumps, Matt woke up. "Where are you off to so early in the morning?"

"Shopping."

Conveniently forgetting that he'd contributed money toward a new designer bag, he gave her a look of displeasure.

Regina smiled at her husband. "I'm going out to get something for dinner. I thought we'd have a candlelight dinner at home tonight. Are you in the mood for some seafood lasagna, sautéed vegetables, homemade rolls, and your favorite…peach cobbler?"

Matt sat up, grimacing as he scratched his head. "I'm not sure if I'm going to be home for dinner, baby. The workload is really piling up and we didn't finish up everything last night. That crew of mine does as little as possible and you know what they say, if you want something done…"

"I know, Matt. But they're paid to do a job. You shouldn't have to pick up behind them."

"That's true, but I can't make those good-for-nothings take pride in a business that doesn't belong to them. Look, I'm the one who has to take the flack if folks come to work on Monday morning and find trash overflowing and floors unpolished. But don't worry, baby. I've already started a proposal to get some more help. Things will be back to normal before you know it."

Regina looked crestfallen. She was really looking forward to spending some quality time with her husband. She was looking forward to putting on some sexy lingerie and convincing him, despite his old-fashioned morality, to nibble on her clit. The thought made her laugh. But really, if he couldn't get the job done the traditional way, maybe he should consider giving her oral sex. Hell, it was worth a try. And after twenty years of marriage, she felt that perhaps she could let go of her own inhibitions and learn how to give her husband head. Drastic measures were necessary; their sex life was a disgrace.

"Oh yeah, I almost forgot..."

She peered at him.

"Uh...you wouldn't happen to still have that money I gave you the other day, would you?"

"Sure, why?"

"I'm running short on cash. I didn't realize a business owner should try to stay ahead of his taxes. My accountant said I need to pay the IRS a little something every quarter, that way I won't get all jammed up at tax time."

She'd looked forward to spending an evening with Matt. Resignedly, Regina opened her purse and gave him the four fifties.

Trying to figure out what to do with her unplanned free time, Regina sat on the bed, elbows resting on her knees, with her hands cupping her face.

In a flash, Matt was up and dressed. Before she even gathered her thoughts and found the words to ask Matt if they could possibly plan something for later on that evening, Matt kissed her on the cheek and galloped down the stairs.

It was a well-cared-for apartment complex. Compared to the raunchy neighborhood where he picked his crew up, the complex's location off Providence Road, on East Twenty-fourth Street in Chester, was idyllic. They were shown two apartments. The one-bedroom was more fitting with Matt's budget, but Onika insisted on the more expensive of the two—the one with a den and a view of the park and a running stream.

Matt filled out the paperwork, paid the deposit, and was told he could pick up the keys on Monday.

"Is my name gonna be on the lease?" Onika wanted to know.

The rental agent looked puzzled. "Why, no. The name on the lease is the person with the credit rating." The woman looked at Matt. "Do you want me to run a credit check on your…"

"My wife," Matt said, his face revealing his discomfort. Onika's mouth opened in wide protest, but Matt shot her a look.

The rental agent hit some keys on a computer. "Your name?" she asked Onika.

"Regina Wheeler," Matt blurted and then provided his wife's social security number. Eyeing Onika suspiciously, the woman keyed in the numbers.

After a few moments, she said, "Okay, you have A-1 credit, Mrs…uh…Wheeler, and of course your name can be added to the lease."

"Mrs. Wheeler," Onika repeated with mocking laughter. "Yeah, it's cool to be on the lease and everything, but y'all better make sure you cut an extra key. As long as I have my own key, I don't care about the lease. Feel me?" she asked the befuddled rental agent. The agent nodded uncertainly.

Before leaving the rental office, Matt made a few polite parting remarks. Impatiently, Onika looked at the time, displayed in colorful digital numbers that lit up the screen of her new device. "I'm ready when you are," she said, screwing up her lips.

Matt gave the agent a limp smile and hurried Onika out of the office.

They left the building and walked toward the parking lot. "Damn, Mr. Wheeler. You know we still gotta go look at some furniture. Why you gotta be bustin' it up with that white heifer like she's somebody important. She ain't nobody; she just works there."

"I was being polite, Onika. What's wrong with your attitude lately? You've been so edgy and unpleasant. What happened to my sweetie pie?" He gazed at her with a mixture of confusion and adoration. His fingers sought to lift her chin affectionately, but Onika dodged his touch by sharply turning her head.

"I saw a bangin' bedroom set. It was advertised at a furniture store at the Tri-State Mall in Claymont, Delaware," she said with a happy lilt to her voice. "They don't have state taxes in Delaware, so you can probably save a stack. Wanna go check it out?"

Matt looked troubled. "Not today, baby girl. I just put a lot of money down on our place, and..."

"I thought it was *my* place," she interrupted.

"You know what I mean. It's your place, but I'll be spending a lot of time there with you."

"So, whatchu saying? You just gonna pop over anytime you feel like it?"

"No, not at all. I'd never invade your privacy like that. I'd always call or make arrangements ahead of time."

"So, you won't need that extra key, will you?"

Hurt, Matt winced. "I'd like to have a key, Onika. Suppose something happens...an emergency or something? Don't you think it would be a good idea for me to have the extra key? And as I said, I would never use it without your permission."

Onika murmured unhappily.

"Anything special you'd like to do with the rest of our day, sweetheart?" he asked, putting his arm around her.

"I told you what I want to do," she snapped. "I guess you expect me to sleep on the floor or something."

"Onika," Matt said patiently. "You'll have a bedroom set. I know some places that sell like-new furniture. I'll pick up a set for you next week."

"Why can't I pick out my own bedroom set? And what makes you think I wanna sleep on something that a bunch of other niggas been sleeping on? I don't want no used damn furniture. You're full of shit. You promised to give me a couple hundred for pocket money, now you crying broke and can't even buy me new furniture."

"Baby—" Matt reached for her but Onika jerked away.

Conveying her displeasure, she poked out her lips and pulled out her cell. "Yo, let me speak to that new blackout—um, what's her name?" Onika looked upward as she tried to recall the blackout's name. "You know," she spat into the phone, sounding annoyed that the person on the other end of the phone didn't immediately provide her with the name of the person she wanted to talk to. "The one who came in last night dressed in them hot-ass winter clothes." Onika giggled at the memory. "Nicole! Yeah, that's her name." Onika cut an eye at Matt, who looked unhappy and confused. "She ain't there? Where the hell she at? Oh, my bad. I forgot the blackouts had to go to four meetings today. Well, what time do you expect her to be back? Oh, okay. Well, do me a favor?" Onika yelled into the phone. "I'll be back at the house in a short. Tell Nicole I need her to do my hair." She ended the call, and then tucked the cell inside her purse. She gave Matt a smug smile.

"Since you can't afford to get my hair done, I made other arrangements. One of the blackouts is gonna do my hair. But I have to wash and condition it myself, so let's go. Drop me off at the womens' house," she said snidely.

Matt glanced down at his watch anxiously. "You're ready to leave me already? I made plans to spend the day with you."

"Sorry," she said dryly. She smoothed back the coarse hair at her temples. "I need a perm. I can't go around another day with my hair looking like this."

"If I give you the money to get your hair done, can you spend some time with me?" he asked pitifully.

She pondered the question. "I guess...but I'm gonna need eighty dollars."

"Eighty dollars! Onika, my wife only spends fifty dollars at the hair salon."

Onika shot Matt a look that made him recoil. "I don't give a fuck what your dumb-ass wife spends on her hair. She's probably getting something fucked up like a press and curl. And don't be comparing me to no other bitches. My 'do costs eighty dollars. Either you got it or you don't. You told me I was getting two hundred dollars, you should be glad I'm only hitting you up for eighty." She rolled her eyes. "Fuck it. Keep your damn money." Onika turned abruptly and started walking fast toward Matt's car.

"Onika!" he yelled.

Onika ignored him and stomped toward the car.

"Onika! Baby!" he yelled louder as hastened his steps to catch up with her.

Onika suddenly stopped and jerked around angrily. "Stop fuckin' calling my name all loud out in public. I thought we was supposed to be keeping this shit on the low." She sucked her teeth and then shot an ominous look at the upper windows of the apartment building. Matt followed her upward gaze.

"Nigga's up there peepin' this shit," she warned him. "They looking at your dumb ass, acting all stupid and shit..." Onika paused, grimacing in disgust. "Running after me; screaming my name, puttin' me on blast." She blew out a disgusted burst of air. "Damn, nigga, you need to get a fuckin' grip."

CHAPTER 9

Onika's pleasant disposition had changed overnight. Matthew Wheeler had never experienced such glaring disrespect, not from a man and certainly not from a woman. But what could he do? She had a hold on him and she knew it. She was the only woman who could get his dick hard. He needed her. He'd just have to have a stiff upper lip and endure her volcanic tantrums.

Onika leaned impatiently against the passenger door, shifting her weight from one foot to the other—huffing and puffing as she waited for Matt to unlock the door. Instead of doing so, he approached her. There was a long silence as he stood next to her. He was in a quandary as to how to improve her mood and get her to spend some time with him.

She gave a low hollow laugh. "You gonna unlock the door or are we just gonna stand out here like two assholes?"

Matt had never felt so helpless in his life. He didn't want to take Onika back to the Recovery House, but he couldn't afford to keep doling out cash. It seemed no matter what he did, it wasn't enough; she always wanted more. He thought he earned enough money to afford a girl on the side, but with Onika's ever-increasing needs, he was going to have to triple his income to keep her happy.

Resignedly, Matt relented. He gave Onika two of the fifty-dollar bills he'd gotten from his wife earlier that morning. "You hungry, baby—wanna stop somewhere and get something to eat?" he asked meekly.

She shook her head adamantly. "Hell no!" She peered at the money. "Now I can afford to go to a real hair stylist instead of letting that new blackout mess up my hair with a bad perm. I gotta call the beauty salon and see what time my hair stylist can fit me in." She pulled out the cell and started pushing numbers. Matt looked close to tears as he listened to her make arrangements to visit the salon.

"She can see me in an hour," she said brightly, as if she were giving Matt good news. "Can you give me a ride to Yeadon?"

Matt covered Onika's hand with his and gently squeezed it. "I thought we were going to spend some quality time together. Can't you push your appointment back a few hours?"

"My stylist don't play that shit," she snapped, pulling her hand from his grasp. "I'm lucky she can squeeze me in with such short notice." Then, noticing Matt's woebegone expression, Onika softened her tone. "Look, we ain't got a whole lot of time to get a room, but I know a spot not too far from here in Crozier Park. It's real private; nobody will bother us there."

Matt squinted skeptically. "You want to have sex outside in the park?"

"No, asshole. I was talking about doing it in the car."

Matt winced at being called an asshole, but he took the insult without comment. His eyes traveled over her attire. "But you're wearing jeans. How will we manage?" he asked, apprehensive.

Onika arched a brow. "Damn, why you gotta question everything? You're really fuckin' up my mood." She sucked her teeth.

"For your information—" Onika paused, and then sighed heavily—"there's a little split in the crotch of my jeans." She waited for Matt to respond. He gave her a blank look. "Let me break it down for you…if you promise to buy me another pair, I'll rip the split wide open."

He was speechless. Onika's demand for more money was outrageous. She was really working him over and he was helpless to deny her.

"Why you acting all quiet? If I rip open my jeans, are you gonna buy me another pair?"

"Maybe you shouldn't rip your good jeans…" he stammered, hoping he sounded concerned about destroying a perfectly good pair of jeans when he was actually desperate to hold on to his remaining cash.

"They're already ripped, dickhead," she screamed at him. "You're so fuckin' stingy. Too cheap to buy me a twenty-dollar pair of jeans. I don't need this bullshit. Open the fuckin' door," she shouted and then folded her long arms defiantly.

"Onika. I don't appreciate the language you're using. I was only suggesting that it would be a waste of money to deliberately destroy your clothing. I don't mind buying another pair but it seems an unnecessary cost when you can easily pull your pants down."

"Why should I pull them down? It ain't like you gonna fuck me or nothing. All you can do is eat pussy. I was trying to make it convenient for you. But you don't appreciate nothing. Shit, I was prepared to let you eat my pussy for an hour. Well, maybe not a whole hour because I gotta get my hair done, but I was gonna let you suck on it for at least a half-hour or so. But fuck it, you obviously don't like the way my stuff tastes." She spun around and faced the passenger door. "Open the fuckin' door and take me back to the Recovery House," she exploded as she yanked on the door handle.

If he took Onika back to the womens' house, he'd end up with nothing to show for the money he'd already given her. Not to mention the down payment he'd put on the apartment. Realizing it was in his best interest to give her twenty dollars more, Matt reached in his pocket and produced a crinkled bill. "Here, baby. Here's some more money."

"I don't want it," she said with her back to him. "You get on my nerves so bad, I swear to God, you make me want to get high again."

Her threat was effective. Matt approached her from behind and pushed the twenty into the back pocket of her jeans. He pressed up against her lean buttocks and whispered in her ear, "When I get my tongue inside those jeans, I'm going to show you how much I love the way you taste."

Onika spun around. "You're so good to me. I'm sorry I cussed at you, Mr. Wheeler. I got a real bad temper. But from now on, I promise, I'm gonna try my best to keep it in check."

"It's okay, baby. I know you been through a lot in your young life. Kicking a drug habit and staying straight can't be easy. If I was giving you the kind of sex you deserve you wouldn't get so frustrated." Matt squeezed Onika's arm reassuringly. "Until I start satisfying you like a real man, you have my permission to lash out at me. I can hold up against a little profanity. I'd rather you curse at me than take out your frustration by getting high again."

Onika looked absolutely gleeful. "You don't mind if I cuss you out from time to time?"

Matt shook his head solemnly.

"For real, Mr. Wheeler?"

"You can cuss me out if you need to, baby," he said in a martyred tone.

Onika squealed in delight. "You're so understanding, Mr. Wheeler. See, now you're giving me something I can work with. I can't be keeping my emotions all pent up inside. When I get mad, I gotta get shit off my chest."

Pleased that Onika no longer seemed angry, Matt added, "I respect your honesty, Onika."

She sighed wistfully. "Maybe it's the freak in me, but for some reason, my pussy got all hot and bothered when you said you want me to cuss you out until you start fucking me like a real man."

He hadn't actually said he *wanted* her to belittle him with profanity, but he didn't bother to correct Onika. Hopefully, after a long sip of her juices, he'd be able to sustain a mighty erection and then he'd show her who really wore the pants.

After Matt unlocked the door, Onika eagerly slid into the passenger seat.

"You really scared me, baby."

Confused, Onika squinted at him.

"I shouldn't have hesitated when you expressed the desire to make love in the park. It's clear that I'm going to have to act more spontaneous. I'm going to have to stop behaving like an old man." He shook his head ruefully.

"You don't have to step your game up, Mr. Wheeler. I like you just the way you are," she said, giving him a tolerant smile.

"But you admitted that it bothers you that I've yet to make love to you the way you deserve."

Onika shook her head. "I was talkin' shit because I was mad. I don't think nobody's dick can make me cum the way your tongue does."

Matt brightened visibly. "That makes me feel slightly better. But I want to make love to you, Onika. A man shouldn't have to rely on oral skills to keep his woman happy."

A spark of sudden anger flashed in Onika's eyes. "Look, I already said I was happy. Your dick issues ain't my problem. Now if you don't wanna eat no more pussy just say so!"

"Baby," Matt said softly, cajolingly, and then patted her arm. "I love performing oral sex on you." He chuckled suddenly. "I tell myself that your juices give me youth and stamina."

Onika's sour expression morphed to a beaming smile. "Get outta here." She sounded flattered. "You really think I got some youth juice up in my pussy?"

Matt nodded. "You don't realize it, but my penis gets as hard as iron. I'm like a horny eighteen-year-old when I have your taste in my mouth. Nobody, not even my wife, can make me feel as youthful and virile as you do."

"That's whassup, Mr. Wheeler," Onika said, beaming with pride. "So, look..." her voice trailed off as she stared into space.

"What?" Matt asked.

"On Monday while the crew is hard at work, you and me gon' sneak off and jet back to my new apartment. If you want me to, I can sit on your face and let you stick your tongue in my hole for the whole shift," she offered.

The promise of unlimited access to her snatch and its sweet elixir gave Matt a rush of warmth. In fact, he could feel his member stiffening at the very thought of giving Onika a serious tongue-job. Excited, he started the car and swung out of the lot.

A few minutes later, Matt pulled into a secluded area in the park. He felt conspicuous in broad daylight, but Onika assured him that nobody ever ventured into the area. He wanted to ask her how she knew with such certainty, but decided he didn't really want to know the answer.

She tumbled into the backseat. Like a contortionist, she pulled up both legs and pressed them into her chest. She didn't have on panties, and her vagina was fully visible and accessible through the split in the crotch of her jeans.

The sight was so erotic, blood instantly rushed to Matt's shaft and it was harder than ever before. Afraid he'd lose his erection, he decided to forgo cunnilingus. He quickly unzipped his pants and released his penis. Seeing his member fully erect was such a beautiful sight, he couldn't help but admire it.

"Come on, Mr. Wheeler, whatchu waiting for?" Onika shouted impatiently.

Instantly, his dick went soft in his hand. Not wanting to incur Onika's ire if he dawdled trying to get his dick back up, he resignedly positioned his head between her legs and began to gently lick her labia. If he worked slowly, perhaps the hard-on would return.

Onika squirmed away. "Whatchu doin'? The way you licking my coochie feels nasty and creepy as shit. Stop playing around, Mr. Wheeler. Eat my pussy like you got some damn sense," she shouted and then banged her kneecaps hard against the sides of his head. His eardrums rang from the sudden blow.

Her abuse had escalated from verbal to physical, but Matt accepted it as just punishment. A young girl deserved a man who could lay heavy pipe, not an impotent, practically middle-aged loser.

Determinedly, he stiffened his tongue and probed long and hard, until he felt the heat from her pussy warming his tongue. As spasms jerked her body, he separated her labia and slipped his limp penis into the gooey warmth. It would have been thrilling to be able to drive his dick inside deeply, but it was too soft to achieve proper penetration.

Rubbing the head of his dick into her creamy cum, he became surprisingly rigid. The time had come to fuck Onika's brains out. Elated, Matt attempted to penetrate. But he was so excited he quickly climaxed, too quickly to experience any pleasure from the experience. He was so disappointed, he punched the back of the driver's seat.

"Goddamn. You ain't gotta take out your frustration on the car seat." Onika glared at him, then reached her lanky body over the passenger seat to grab the box of tissues that Matt kept in the glove compartment.

"I let you bust a nut but you still gotta act like a damn asshole," she mumbled as she used a wad of tissues to wipe between her legs.

He couldn't blame Onika for her complete loss of respect for him. He wasn't handling his business right. If he could maintain an erection and give her the hard dick a man was supposed to provide, certainly he'd regain the respect she once had for him. Until then, he'd have to accept that he deserved her contempt.

His wife's suggestion that he think about getting a prescription for Viagra was starting to sound appealing.

CHAPTER 10

While her husband had decided to pass up his day off to labor at his cleaning business, Regina had spent an entire Saturday relaxing in bed, indulging her sensuality. Private sessions with her new sex toy had become more than just a pastime. Each time Regina eased the vibrating penile object into her hot spot, she became more attached, more dependent on the mechanical device.

The need to relieve her sexual tension was bordering on obsession. A magnificent obsession! Oddly, she now considered her husband a great humanitarian—a living saint. By leaving the house to work on his day off, Matt had inadvertently provided her with extended time and privacy to discover her G-spot. And after that great discovery, she was certain her life would never be quite the same.

Brushing back damp ringlets, the result of intense and repeated orgasms, Regina traipsed down the basement stairs and carefully concealed the object of her obsession. She gave the vibrator one last look before nestling it amid her secret stash. Hopefully her horniness had been satiated for the day, and she'd have the willpower to get through the preparation of her husband's dinner without interruption.

But it was only wishful thinking. Five minutes into chopping vegetables and boiling water for pasta, she felt the beginnings of a gentle stirring between her legs. She tried her best to ignore it, but the mild arousal began building again until it became incessant hot pangs, insisting she stop everything. Entranced, seeming without a will of her own, she responded to the sex call and obediently covered the pots and pans she'd been tending to and turned off the burners.

But before rushing back down the basement stairs to rip the vibrator from its hiding place, she managed to come out of her sex-induced stupor long enough to call Matt. She needed to gauge how much time she had before he came bursting through the front door.

Matt answered his cell sounding breathless.

"Hi, honey. Where are you?"

"Still working. I'll be here for another hour or so," he said, sounding both annoyed and distracted.

Good! "Okay, I'll see you when you get home," Regina replied pleasantly. She had at least another hour of leisure time. She had to hand it to herself, she was fast on her feet. It took some really quick thinking for her to postpone the masturbation session to determine Matt's whereabouts. God forbid Matt should arrive home and find her lying on her back with her legs agape, moaning in time with the low hum of the battery-operated dick.

After a powerful orgasm, it took a moment for Regina's heart rate to slow down. Lying in bed, spent and dreamy-eyed, it seemed unfair that she had to come out of her comfort zone and trudge back down to the basement to get rid of the evidence. *Evidence of what?* she asked herself as indignation propelled her to bolt upright. The only *evidence* in her bedroom was the fact that her husband was terrible in bed! It would serve Matt right if he discovered the imitation dick that was keeping his sex-starved wife satisfied.

In her mind, Matt had been quickly demoted from saint to sinner. She'd asked him to get professional help and he'd refused. Selfish and insensitive, he'd never provided any emotional support after they'd lost their son. He had his nephew. She was left hanging, alone with her unresolved grief.

Exploring her sexuality was an awakening. What the hell did she need Matt for? His money? What a laugh. All his extra money went into his business and she could afford to support herself. It was time to stop accepting their problem. She absolutely deserved a healthy sex life. Feeling sexually attractive was an essential part of a woman's existence.

Matt, she decided with a sigh, was on very shaky ground.

As Regina flirted with the thought of leaving her husband, she heard his car pulling into the driveway. But she wasn't as brave as she'd thought. Instead of meeting him at the door and brazenly waving the plastic dick in his face, she stuffed it in her lingerie drawer.

And as far as asking for a divorce…it would be totally out of character for her to make such a brash move. No, she'd have to give the subject a lot more thought. *Calm down,* she told herself. The multiple orgasms were making her lose her mind. Smiling a secret smile, Regina glanced in the mirror and ran a brush through her hair and then went downstairs to finish preparing dinner.

In the confines of his small room, Cochise completed the last set of pushups. He was strong as an ox. *Cock strong!* Yeah, that's what they said about men like him. Being cock strong and furious was a lethal combination, which was why he'd walked away from the dude who had accused him of stealing his cigarettes. Cochise didn't even smoke. Had he gripped the brother by the neck the way he imagined himself doing, that man would be dead right now. But Cochise had wisely walked away. His accuser was new in the mens' house and had mistaken Cochise's quiet demeanor and reddish skin tone for someone who was on some punk-ass shit. Yeah, Cochise had walked away. It was a slow walk with a defiant swagger and by now the big-mouth dude had been schooled by his housemates that everyone in the Recovery House gave Cochise mad respect.

Drenched in sweat, he yanked the soggy bandana from around his head, allowing a curtain of shimmering blue-black hair to fall past his shoulders. With a hand towel, he dried his hair, face, neck, and massive, iron-hard shoulders. He pulled a dry bandana from the top drawer, gathered up his heavy hair, and tied it back from his face before beginning ten sets of one-arm pushups.

"*Cock strong,*" he repeated with a grunt as he lifted his two-hundred-and-fifty-pound muscular frame with one sweat-streaked arm. Many of the recovering females who lived in the womens' house frequently hit on Cochise, boldly offering sex, but he politely declined. He thought he'd been exercising sound judgment when he got involved with Shawna but their "arrangement" ended on a horrible note. He knew for certain that getting involved with another addict could only be a recipe for disaster.

His thoughts returned to Shawna. He shook his head, sorry that he'd hurt her, disappointed with himself for not recognizing that she'd wanted more than he was able to give. No more friends with benefits, he sternly told himself. One day he'd meet someone special. He knew Tierra would want him to fall in love again. But he wasn't ready. So, in the meantime, he'd deal with his sex drive by beating his meat. Yeah, until he was completely free of his demons, he'd have to get used to taking matters into his own hands. Literally.

CHAPTER 11

Although the rental agent had given both Matt and Onika a key, the moment they left the office Matt dutifully turned his key over to Onika, placing it in her outstretched hand. Like a lovesick puppy, he followed her from room to room. The place had been freshly painted. A paint-spattered metal chair, two empty cans of paint, a tarp, duct tape, and masking tape were left in a clutter inside the kitchen. "These mufuckas must be crazy leaving all this bullshit for us to clean," Onika complained. "You need to deduct half of next month's rent! Humph!" She placed a hand on her lean hip. "I don't know who they think they fuckin' with."

"What do you want to do with the den, baby girl?" Matt changed the subject, hoping to improve Onika's mood.

"I'm turning the den into a game room," she said, suddenly cheerful. "I want a PlayStation3 and a sixty-inch plasma screen up on the wall. This room is gon' be red and black. Red walls, black leather swivel chairs, and we gonna have to pull up these cheap-ass rugs and lay down some thick-ass, ruby-red carpets."

"I don't think we can paint the walls or pull up the carpets," Matt said worriedly. "We can't deface the property. I'd have to pay through the nose if we put holes in the wall trying to mount a large TV—"

"Whatever," she said, cutting Matt off. "What they don't know won't hurt 'em. Besides, can't nobody tell me what to do in my own crib," Onika complained, her lips protruding.

"You're right, baby," Matt cajoled. He reached for her hand. "Why don't you take your clothes off so you can ride my face?"

Eyes widened in disbelief, Onika reared back. She placed a fist on her slender hip. "You must be out of your muthafuckin' mind! I'm not getting down on the floor with your dumb ass."

"What's wrong, baby? You promised."

"Yeah, but I thought I'd have a bed or something in here. I ain't doing shit until we pick up some furniture. And not no used furniture, either," she added with disdain.

"Onika. I'm not a rich man," Matt said, carefully monitoring his tone. "I can't afford to buy brand-new furniture just yet. Be reasonable, baby."

Onika folded her arms. "No! Ain't nothin' to be reasonable about. Ain't no furniture up in this dip. Ain't no dishes, no forks, no spoons..." Onika sucked her teeth. "We ain't got nothin' up in here."

"I'm sorry," Matt said miserably. "You're right. I should have had more foresight." He tried to embrace her.

"Don't touch me! You get on my fuckin' nerves," Onika fumed. In a matter of seconds, she balled a fist, drew her arm back, and hooked Matt in his left eye. The sound echoed in the empty apartment. The unexpected power in her small, angry fist knocked his Eagles cap askew.

"Ugh!" Matt grunted. One hand reflexively covered the injured eye. The other hand quickly twisted around the brim of the worn green cap.

"See that shit," she said, huffing and puffing. "See what you made me do? That's what you get for putting your hands on me when I'm mad."

"I'm all right. It's okay, baby," Matt said as he moved quickly to the bathroom to inspect the damage.

Looking more interested than concerned, Onika followed Matt into the bathroom. "Aw, it ain't nothing," she said with a *tsk* as she stood behind him and spoke to his unblemished reflection.

"You're right," he said, sounding relieved. "But I should probably put some ice on it to prevent any swelling." Matt turned to go to the kitchen.

"Ain't no ice in there," Onika muttered knowingly.

In the kitchen, Matt opened the freezer and found three plastic trays filled with ice.

"Oh, all right," Onika exclaimed, surprised. "Well, whatchu gonna put it in?"

Matt looked around the empty kitchen, removed his cap and scratched his head.

"Don't worry, Mr. Wheeler. I got something for you to wrap it in." Onika's tone was suddenly soft. Forgiving. And seductive.

Before Matt could respond, Onika pulled down her jeans. Stripped down to a T-shirt and a pair of black panties, she stood with her back pressed against one of the bare kitchen walls. Curling the soft black fabric past her hips, she stepped out of the panties and offered them to Matt. "Here you go," she said wearing a sly grin.

Matt took the panties. He sniffed the crotch and deeply inhaled her feminine scent. Like one of Pavlov's dogs, Matt licked his lips and began to salivate at the sight of Onika's pubis. No longer interested in giving himself first aid, he shoved the ice tray back inside and slammed the freezer door. "Can I taste it, baby? Just one taste?" he pleaded.

A lustful look flashed across Onika's face. "I'm not even gonna front, Mr. Wheeler. Like I told you, I got a lot of freak in me." With her penetrating eyes fastened to his, she ran her middle finger over her clit and then slipped it inside. After several thrusts, she held up the glistening finger. "See how my pussy acts when you make me mad?"

"Oh yeah, baby. I see." He looked at her finger longingly. "Can I taste it?"

Onika extended her finger, offering it to Matt. Then she suddenly snatched it back, taunting him, forcing him to stretch his neck and lengthen his tongue to lick the sticky moisture.

Dipping her long finger in and out of her overly moist pussy, Onika finger-fed Matt her juices. Anxiously, his hand brushed against his crotch, unzipped his pants, and snaked inside his fly. Closing his palm around his erection, Matt stroked his dick as he sucked Onika's creamy finger.

"Eric called," Regina told Matt after he got in bed beside her.

"Damn!" Matt groaned. "I promised to drop off the money he needs for his senior class dues."

"Yes, that's what he said. He seemed pretty upset. I told him you've been so busy lately, it probably slipped your mind."

"*Busy* is putting it mildly. Trying to get a good day's work out of my crew is like pulling teeth. Not only do I have to pick them up and drop them off; I have to babysit those lazy grown men...." Matt shook his head in irritation. "I have to go behind them and make sure the job is done right. Running a business is hard work.

Eric's going to have to understand, I don't have a lot of free time or money to throw around."

"Well, Matt you did promise to give him the money," Regina said logically.

"True. Would you call him for me tomorrow and tell him I'll write a check and send it to his school?"

"Sure. Speaking of calling Eric, I asked him how he liked his new phone." With her brow crinkled in confusion, Regina met her husband's eyes. "Eric said you hadn't given him a new phone. He didn't know what I was talking about."

Matt returned his wife's confused gaze. Unaccustomed to lying on a regular basis, and unable to concoct a quick excuse, Matt was briefly stumped. His mind raced, trying to come up with a plausible explanation. "Oh!" he finally said with a relieved chuckle. "I forgot to mention it; I returned the phone. Got my money back. You gave me something to think about when you said I spoil that boy. Eric's never going to learn the meaning of responsibility if I keep giving him everything he asks for. He's got to be better prepared for the future. I don't want him to turn out like any of those worthless morons who work for me."

Regina looked at Matt, surprised. For the past ten years she'd been telling Matt that he spoiled his nephew rotten. Now, though he hadn't actually admitted that it was wrong to cave in and give his nephew everything he wanted, he'd taken her words into consideration and had quietly returned the cell phone. It felt like a victory. Regina felt a ripple of hope.

"I'm tired," Matt said stiffly. He turned and switched off the lamp on his side of the bed. After plumping his pillow and snuggling into a comfortable position, he reminded Regina, "Don't forget to call Eric tomorrow."

A few minutes later, as Matt snored next to her, Regina reached over and turned off the light from the matching lamp on her side of the bed. In deep thought, she gazed into the darkened bedroom. She'd give her marriage one last chance. In a day or so, she'd gather her courage and give Matt an ultimatum. She wouldn't beat around the bush or sugarcoat her words. She'd speak bluntly, tell him straight out that she was at her sexual peak and that after taking matters into her own hands, she'd finally experienced the toe-curling, body-thrashing, heart-pounding orgasm that she'd heard so much about. Now that she knew that she was fully capable of reaching a climax, she'd let him know that she was no longer willing to spend the rest of her life locked in a passionless marriage, aching for sexual release.

If he refused to get help for his dysfunction, she'd have no choice but to end their twenty-year marriage.

CHAPTER 12

Theo was drinking on the job again. Cochise had smelled it on his breath, but he'd pretended not to notice. Cochise wrapped his large hands around the handle of the automatic floor scrubber and pushed the two-hundred-and-fifty-pound machine over the tiled fifth-floor corridor with ease. He reminded himself that Theo's drinking was none of his business. If the boss didn't care, why should he give a fuck? It wasn't like he was paid extra money to supervise while Mr. Wheeler was laying up in a hotel somewhere or, if the gossip was true, chillin' in the apartment he had hooked up for Onika. Shit, the way things had been going down lately, Cochise would be lucky to get paid the regular wages Mr. Wheeler owed him.

"Damn, I forgot to bring the payment vouchers," Mr. Wheeler had told the three-man work crew when he'd dropped them off at the site in Germantown. "I'll take care of you fellas tomorrow," he assured them. It was the second time that week he'd claimed to have forgotten the vouchers. The same thing had happened the week before. The workers didn't get their cash stipend if they didn't turn the pay vouchers in to the house manager at the Recovery House.

"Oh yeah," Mr. Wheeler said, pressing his fingers against his forehead in thought. "Something's come up." He solemnly shook his head, his expression grave. "I've got a little problem, have to make a quick run. I'm gonna need you guys to handle things while I'm gone. I should be back in a couple of hours."

Mr. Wheeler knew damn well that the only problem his married ass had was finding time to spend with his new jump-off. Onika no longer bothered to show up for work, but Cochise would bet a month's salary that Mr. Wheeler was making sure she got her pay vouchers.

Cochise shook his head. Mr. Wheeler should be ashamed of himself—knocking boots with a troubled young girl he was supposed to be helping.

"Cochise! Yo, man, you better come downstairs."

Cochise bristled at the sound of Theo's slurred voice. A jolt of annoyance ran through him as he caught a whiff of the smell of cheap liquor that permeated the corridor.

With restrained anger, Cochise looked over his shoulder. Theo could hardly stand up straight. No way could he walk a straight line or pass a Breathalyzer test if he had to. Cochise turned around and faced Theo. "Man, you're drunk as shit. Why you fuckin' yourself up like this? You tryin' to get fired?"

"I ain't gon' lie, man. I had a little taste, but I can hold my liquor; I'm not intoxicated," Theo told Cochise, speaking slowly, as he tried to control his slurred speech.

"What's going on downstairs?" Cochise asked, unable to hide his irritation at being called away from his work to give assistance to someone who had created a mess due to his drunkenness. He blew out an exasperated breath. Mr. Wheeler didn't pay him enough to clean up behind drunk-ass Theo. Mr. Wheeler was going to have to get his shit together and handle the business he was contracted to handle or Cochise was going to be looking for another job real soon.

"It ain't me, man. It's old man Faison. He's breathing real hard, acting like he's about to have a heart attack or something."

"Oh, damn!" Cochise let go of the handles of the automatic scrubber and ran toward the stairwell. Staggering, Theo trailed behind him. His boots pounded against the concrete stairs as Cochise took them two at a time. He made it to the ground floor in less than two minutes. When he passed through the door that opened into the lobby, a cold chill ran down his spine. He was greeted by the foreboding sight of boots with the toes pointed upward. Mr. Faison lay prone in the center of the carpeted floor of the lobby.

"He dead?" Theo asked in a whisper.

Kneeling beside Mr. Faison, Cochise searched for a pulse. "He's alive but he's gonna need an ambulance."

"Mr. Faison! Get up, man. Mr. Faison!" Theo shouted.

"Man, stop all that screaming and call fuckin' 911." Cochise lifted Mr. Faison's head from the floor. He'd heard about people choking on their own saliva and hoped to keep his co-worker from asphyxiating while they waited for help.

"I ain't got no cell phone, Cochise."

"Stop playin', Theo. Use one of the office phones."

"Don't you know CPR or something? I don't think Mr. Wheeler would want—"

"Fuck that pussy," Cochise bellowed. Deciding to make the call himself, he rested Mr. Faison's head on the floor.

When his head touched the cool tiled floor, Mr. Faison's eyes popped open. With a questioning expression, he looked from Cochise to Theo. "What happened?"

"You passed out," Theo informed him.

Cochise nodded in agreement.

"Yeah, we thought you was dead, man," Theo continued. "I was just getting ready to call 911."

"I'm all right," Mr. Faison said, though he was breathing hard and struggling to sit upright.

"Naw, you ain't all right. Nobody passes out for nothing. You need to get checked out at the hospital," Cochise said firmly.

"It's my blood sugar, man. I got diabetes. I'll be all right after I get my prescription refilled."

Cochise gave the older man a long, incredulous look. "Then get your shit refilled. Whatchu tryin' to do—kill yourself?"

"No, man. It ain't that," Mr. Faison said, reaching out for Cochise to give him a hand. "The medical coverage we got only pays for about two weeks' worth of pills. I gotta come outta pocket to get the pills for the rest of the month."

Quietly seething, Cochise pulled Mr. Faison to his feet. It was time to confront Mr. Wheeler. That slimy bastard was holding back pay from a man who needed money to pay for his medicine. It wasn't right.

"Get off your feet, man. Fall back. Me and Theo can finish up the lobby for you."

"Say what?" Theo asked, face contorted in disagreement.

Cochise glared at Theo and then pointed to the sofa in the reception area. "Rest yourself over there, Mr. Faison. Like I said, me and Theo gotchu."

A wobbly Mr. Faison flopped down on the sofa and collapsed against the cushion.

"Man, why you volunteer my services? I ain't getting paid to do no extra work," Theo grumbled as he put a fresh plastic liner in the wastebasket.

"Don't worry. We gon' get our money and a little something extra for our trouble. Mr. Wheeler might be taking me for a chump, but trust me, he don't wanna see my bad side," Cochise said, his voice going down an octave.

An hour after the shift ended, there was no sign of Mr. Wheeler. Feeling played by his boss, Cochise quietly seethed while Theo drank openly from a flask.

"I just want to get back to the House so I can lie down," Mr. Faison commented in a weak raspy voice as he struggled to lift himself from a reclined position on the sofa.

Theo threw his head back and took a long, defiant swig from the flask, quickly downing the liquor. He wiped his mouth with the back of his hand and nudged his head toward Mr. Faison. "That man is sick as a dog and the boss got us waiting. It was bad enough that the nigga forgot our pay vouchers, but now he got us stuck all the way the fuck up here in Philly."

"Don't worry about getting back to Chester. I got enough money for the bus ride."

"Bus ride! Man, it's probably gonna take about three or four buses to get from here to Chester," Theo complained.

Cochise nodded. "You right." He slid Theo a twenty. "That should be enough to get you and Mr. Faison back to the House. I'll get at y'all later on tonight. I'm gonna hang around here for a minute. You know…look after the equipment 'til the boss gets back. And then I'm gonna give him a few choice words." Cochise's lips curled into a sneer. "There won't be nothing nice coming outta my mouth." His tone was low and menacing.

CHAPTER 13

"Can I get a smile?" Matt asked Onika after relinquishing his credit card to the sales associate at Vanity Furniture Company.

"Hell no!" Onika turned her nose up as if Matt were stinking up the furniture showroom. "Why you gotta be so damn cheap all the time?"

"Cheap? I just forked over forty-six hundred dollars."

"So what," she snarled. "The man told you he could have the furniture delivered tomorrow morning if you paid a little bit extra."

"Onika, why should I cough up almost three hundred dollars extra when I own a van and have access to a work crew who can deliver the furniture?" Matt asked, trying to appeal to Onika's common sense. "Look, baby. I'll take Cochise and the boys straight to the furniture store when I pick them up tomorrow. We'll get all the furniture in here before I take them to the work site."

Giving Matt a hand flip, Onika snarled, "I'm not tryna hear that shit." Rotating her neck, she continued, "I'm not lettin' your raunchy workers put their hands on my new furniture. I want my shit delivered and set up by professionals." Onika gave a heavy sigh, folded her arms defiantly, and rolled her eyes at Matt. "I can just see trifling-ass Theo and sick old Mr. Faison dropping my shit and fucking it up. And that hateful Cochise..." Onika sucked her teeth. "That evil-ass, Indian-looking mufucka would probably damage my nice furniture just for the hell of it. Fuck you, Mr. Wheeler, and fuck your work crew," Onika said loudly, causing customers and sales associates to rear back in shock.

"Lower your voice, sweetheart," Matt said in a placating tone.

"Fuck you," she shouted with a nasty grimace in an even louder voice. "Take me home, asshole. I don't need your stingy ass. I can get my own goddamn furniture."

Though Onika was lanky with no hips or behind to speak of, it didn't matter to Matt. She was the sexiest woman he had ever encountered. Inexplicably, her anger and her insulting profanity made his small dick lengthen to what felt like at least two more inches as it hardened inside his pants. Without another word, Matt gave Onika a smile of concession. Resignedly, he walked over to the sales counter. "Listen, go ahead and add that delivery charge. My, uh, wife wants to get the furniture delivered tomorrow." Matt and the sales associate gave Onika strained smiles.

Onika put her hand on her hip and glared at the two men. "What y'all lookin' at me for? Y'all need to hurry up and run that credit card. I'm not tryin' to stand around here all day. I got shit to do." She shifted impatiently from one foot to the other and blew out several furious bursts of air.

Matt gave the sales associate an apologetic smile. "Could you speed it up a little, buddy? She's not feeling well. I...uh, have to get her home."

"Sure, no problem." The salesman, apparently unwilling to risk losing the sale, obliged with a widened grin and quickly punched the additional figures into the computer.

Matt revved the engine happily. He'd bought Onika everything she'd asked for and despite the fact that she was sitting next to him looking unpleasant and grumpy, he was sure that when they got back to her apartment, his skillful tongue could lick her into a better mood.

Five minutes after leaving the Claymont, Delaware, mall, they passed the WELCOME TO PENNSYLVANIA sign. Matt smiled to himself. They'd be in Chester soon. After splurging on furniture, he figured he'd earned the right to slip off her jeans and wrap his lips around her tasty clit the moment they stepped inside the apartment.

Onika's cell chimed. "Whaddup?" she barked, holding the handset to her ear. She listened briefly and then turned toward Matt. "Yo, why ain't you get me a Bluetooth. It's annoying holding this thing up to my ear," she complained.

"I'll get you one," Matt sadly obliged.

"So, what's the deal?" she asked, returning to the conversation on the phone.

Matt could hear the urgent, high-pitched vocal tone of a female on the other end of the phone but he couldn't make out what the woman was saying. His instincts told him that the caller's dilemma didn't bode well for him.

Onika snapped her phone shut. "Swing by the womens' Recovery House."

"What for?" he asked, shocked that she would want to go anywhere near that horribly crowded recovery place now that she had her own apartment.

Onika gritted on Matt for a few seconds before speaking. "Not that it's any of your business, but since you gotta be all up in my business, I have to make a quick stop and scoop up my girl, Puddin."

Matt wrinkled his face in annoyance. "I don't have time to provide a taxi service for your drug-addict friends. I have to get back to the job and make sure my crew is doing what they should."

Onika's face turned sour. "Screw you, asshole. You done lost your damn mind. How your old ass gon' be complaining about giving one of my friends a damn ride?"

Matt winced. He'd gotten used to being called an asshole. He'd begun to consider it a term of endearment, but being called *old* stung, particularly when Onika had insisted that she didn't consider him old.

"Onika, I'm still in my thirties. How can you call me old?" Matt asked, deeply wounded.

"Nigga, you pushing forty. I'm only twenty years old. As far as I'm concerned, your ass is old as dirt!"

"Why didn't you admit your feelings in the beginning?" Matt wondered aloud in a pained, cracked voice.

"Yo, I'm not debating the issue. I'm through talkin' to your dumb ass, so drive, nigga. Take me the fuck home. And after you drop me off, you can just keep it movin', 'cause it's gon' be a snowy mufuckin' day in July before I let you taste this good pussy again!"

In a panic, Matt blinked rapidly. Hooked on Onika's womanly flavor, he had to honor her request if he wanted to continue lathering his lips with her nectar. "Okay, I'll pick up your friend," Matt said weakly, giving Onika a pained look.

"Aiight, then. Don't be staring at my face. You better keep your eyes on the road while you driving, nigga."

He quickly refocused his gaze. Worry crinkled his brow. He sure hoped Onika's friend didn't have to travel too far. He hadn't planned on leaving his crew alone for more than an hour or two. Any thoughts of finally penetrating Onika flew out the window. For Matt to maintain an erection would require patience on Onika's part, and she was clearly not feeling tolerant. Once again, Matt would have to jack himself off while dining between her legs.

Looking on the bright side, he thought about tomorrow. He was confident that after the furniture was delivered and set up, Onika would be in the right frame of mind to enjoy intercourse with him.

Pulling off I-95 at the Kerlin Street exit, Matt steered toward the Recovery House.

CHAPTER 14

Matt gave a mental sigh when he spotted the short, light-skinned, barrel-shaped young woman wearing a bright red jacket, black pants, and black ankle boots waiting outside the Recovery House. On the ground beside her boots was an oversized plastic trash bag. The trash bag could only mean trouble for Matt. Apparently, the girl was leaving the House and needed a lift to her next dwelling place.

When Matt pulled his van up to the curb, the roly-poly girl picked up the trash bag and slung it over her shoulder. Approaching the van, looking like Mrs. Santa Claus, Onika's girlfriend waved excitedly. She pulled open the door, climbed inside, and threw her trash bag in the back, and squeezed into the passenger seat with Onika. "Whaddup, Onika!"

"Ain't shit," Onika said dryly.

"Aw, don't be acting all down and out on our first night as roomies."

Matt's jaw dropped. "Onika, what's she—"

"There you go," Onika spat. "Why you gotta be all up in my business?"

"I have a right to know who—"

"Nigga, you ain't got a right to know nothing!"

Puddin laughed. "Damn, Onika, didn't your mother teach you to respect your elders?"

"Yeah, but I only give it when I get it," Onika replied sullenly. "I think it's disrespectful for a nigga to be trying to mind my business."

"You got a point," Puddin agreed.

"I've never disrespected you, Onika," Matt declared, trying to ignore the fact that Puddin had referred to him as an elder. Since when did being thirty-nine years old equate to being an elder? Matt wondered, peeved. "How have I disrespected you?" he persisted.

"Man, would you please pull off from in front of this damn Recovery House," Onika spat. "Shit, I still owe room and board at that bitch."

Matt didn't move. "I asked you how I've ever disrespected you."

Onika sucked her teeth. "Aiight, sit out here if you want to, but if the house manager or somebody tries to come at me, starting some shit about the rent, you better be prepared to come out of your pocket 'cause I ain't giving up a damn thing."

Puddin fell out laughing and slapped Onika's palm. "I know that's right, girl. After they broke up the fight between me and that new chick, Miss Betina gon' tell me I had to go, then she had the nerve to start adding up how much I owed. Now, you know I told her to kiss my big ass."

Onika chuckled briefly and then shot Puddin a curious look. "So, why was you and the new chick fighting?"

Puddin dug inside her purse and opened her palm, revealing a handful of pills. "Bitch snuck some Oxycontin in the house and wasn't trying to share. Now, you know I loves me some Oxy, so I burned her for all her shit. When she tried to accuse me of taking her shit, I busted her mouth."

Smiling, Onika shook her head as if Puddin was a mischievous four-year-old. Matt felt a dislike for Puddin that was so intense, he wanted to pull over and physically toss the pill-popping addict out of his van. He didn't have time to compete for Onika's attention. Now that he'd heard Puddin's story, he knew the pudgy little freeloader would be hanging around forever. He wanted to kiss and make up with Onika as quickly as possible. He didn't have all night. He had a job to do, and men to supervise and transport back to their group home. But with a third wheel in his and Onika's love nest, diffusing his baby girl's anger would take a lot more time and patience than he had tonight. He could only pray that Puddin would take every one of the stolen pills as soon as they returned to the apartment. He hoped Puddin would quickly nod off into oblivion, and give him and his baby girl the privacy they deserved. Who was he kidding? It would be too much like right for Onika's ill-mannered friend to conveniently knock herself out.

Instead of parking, Matt pulled up to the door of building G and sat behind the wheel, allowing the engine to idle while Puddin got out and retrieved her trash bag. Onika sat beside him, silent. "I'm going to give you some time to cool off, baby girl. I'll give you a call early tomorrow morning."

"Oh, it's like that, now?"

"Like what?"

"You just gon' drop me off in front of the crib like you don't give a damn how I feel?"

Matt couldn't win for losing. He was trying to give Onika the space she obviously needed and she still wasn't satisfied. Not knowing what to say, Matt held out his hands and shrugged. He caught a glimpse of Puddin standing at the door of Onika's apartment building and then he felt the buckle of Onika's pocketbook as it crashed against the side of his face.

"What the hell is wrong with you?" he shouted, rubbing his palm across his cheek.

"Why you looking out the window at Puddin? You tryin' to get with my friend?"

"Don't be ridiculous. I just glanced out the window for a moment. I wasn't paying any attention to Puddin." Matt pulled the visor down to check the damage to his face. There was some swelling and redness near his cheekbone, which meant he'd have to concoct a believable story when his wife asked what happened.

There was the sudden sound of Puddin banging on the passenger window. "I know that mufucka didn't put his hands on you!"

Onika slid down the window. "Nah, but I had to crack him upside his head—put that ass in check." She turned to Matt. "Ain't that right, baby?" she asked with a huge grin, as if being smacked with her pocketbook was something he should be proud of.

Matt looked grim. How had he allowed his world to spin so badly out of control? It was possible that Onika was crazy. But what was his excuse for going along with her nuttiness? *I'm pussy whipped*, he solemnly admitted.

"Answer me!" The humor had left Onika's voice.

Not wishing to provoke her again, Matt responded quickly. "Yeah, you keep me in check." *Ugh!* He sounded like a wimp. He rubbed the tender area on his face. The pain was tolerable. He felt more humiliated than physically hurt. He was deeply ashamed that his weakness for Onika had been witnessed by a third party.

He thought he'd made it clear that he didn't mind getting cussed out or smacked around behind closed doors. But now Onika was acting out in front of Puddin. Clearly, Onika was out of control, and Matt didn't know how to rein her back in. He yearned for the sweet, considerate young woman she'd been when he first developed an interest in her.

Matt had to admit, though, that her bad behavior wasn't entirely her fault. He'd spoiled Onika and turned her into the ornery, demanding monster she'd become.

"Here you go." Onika handed Puddin a set of keys. "Apartment 10. Go on in and make yourself at home. There's a little bit of food in the fridge." Onika nodded toward Matt. "This asshole's been bringing me stuff to snack on instead of taking me to the supermarket to do some real grocery shopping."

Matt wanted to defend himself and explain to Onika that with all the furniture shopping they'd done and having to hold down two jobs, he hadn't had the time to take her shopping for groceries. But he didn't dare disagree with Onika. He sat quietly with his head in his hands.

"But I got a little something, something...enough ham and cheese slices to make yourself a couple sandwiches."

"Ham and cheese!" Laughing, Puddin rubbed her plump tummy. "You ain't gotta tell me twice."

"You crazy, girl," Onika replied. "I'm gon sit in the van for a minute. Me and this dickhead gotta have a private conversation."

"Aiight. Holla if you need me," Puddin said, narrowing an eye at Matt.

"So what's the deal with you?" Onika asked Matt after Puddin waddled off.

"Nothing," Matt muttered.

"Nigga please. What's your problem? Spit it out before I smack the shit outta you," she said, raising her hand.

Without a doubt, Matt could physically put a hurting on skinny little Onika if he chose to. But her emotional hold on him was so intense, he feared her. He was afraid of losing the woman whose mistreatment of him served as an aphrodisiac—the woman whose vaginal juices invigorated him like a double dose of Viagra. Matt took a deep breath. "Actually, there is something wrong. For one thing, I wish you wouldn't talk to me with such blatant disrespect when other people are around. It's degrading and I don't appreciate it." Matt took a deep breath and continued. "And secondly, I really wish you wouldn't put your—"

"Secondly, my ass!" Onika gripped Matt by the collar. "I don't give a shit about what you wish!" She tightened her grip and pulled Matt closer, so close, he could feel her warm breath on his face. "Don't make me bash your fuckin' head against that window," she threatened and then released him with a hard shove.

Matt felt the hardening inside his pants. His eyes locked helplessly on Onika's face.

Recognizing the desire that shone in his eyes, Onika patted Matt's crotch and then ran an open palm across the small bulge beneath the fabric. "Aw, my boo might not have to eat no pussy tonight," she said with a smile. "Looks like you're ready to get your fuck on." Onika tenderly stroked the cheek she'd bruised a few minutes ago.

Boo! Matt's heart soared. He'd been feeling insecure lately, but those emotions evaporated as Onika caressed his cheek with one hand and massaged his penis with the other. She couldn't help it if at times her bad temper got out of control. His poor little baby girl had had a hard life. Something really awful must have happened to her while she was out on the streets, he reasoned.

"Come on, Mr. Wheeler. Let's go in the crib so you can put some dick up in this pussy—like a real man."

Matt tried to fuck Onika like a real man, but he couldn't. On the air mattress inside Onika's empty bedroom, Matt's manhood had deflated the moment it touched Onika's pussy. "I can't understand it," he mumbled, pulling desperately on his limp penis. "I'm sorry, baby. You're gonna have to sit on my face until I get myself together," he said regretfully.

"I'm not sitting on nothing but the driver's seat of your van. You're getting on my damn nerves." Onika stood up and held out her hand. "Give me the keys to your van," she demanded.

"Don't be like that, Onika," Matt pleaded. "Come on, baby girl, let me give you some head. Don't you want to cum all over daddy's face?"

"No! I want to cum on a goddamn dick. You got me frustrated," Onika complained as she snatched Matt's pants off the floor and shook his key ring out of a side pocket. "I'm starting to really wonder about you. Whassup, you gay or something, Mr. Wheeler?"

"No!" Matt said vehemently. "You know I'm not a homosexual."

Onika shrugged. "So you say." Dangling Matt's key ring, she added, "I thought you were gonna serve up some hard dick tonight, but it seems like all you wanna do is tongue me to death."

Matt looked miserable. "I thought you enjoyed oral sex with me. Please, baby girl, sit on my face," Matt pleaded and then reached for Onika's hand.

Onika jerked her hand from Matt's. "Puddin!" she shouted at the top of her lungs.

Puddin hustled to the bedroom and burst through the door, clutching an unusually thick ham and cheese sandwich with mayonnaise oozing out the sides. "Did he hit you?" Puddin asked, balling her fists.

"Nah, I do all the hitting in this relationship," Onika boasted. "I need a favor."

"A favor? Girl, I thought you was in here being manhandled. Why you screaming my name while I'm trying to get a grub?" Puddin took a bite of the sandwich and licked a dollop of mayonnaise from her finger. Preoccupied with her appetite, she didn't seem to notice or care that Onika and Matt were naked.

But Matt cared. He was mortified that Onika and her friend were having a casual conversation as if he weren't on the air mattress butt-ass-naked. He desperately wanted to cover his exposed genitals with the sheet. He placed a hand over his private parts and eyed his Eagles cap, wishing it was on his head, concealing his receding hairline. When they'd first entered the bedroom—when Onika's mood was lighter because she thought he'd be able to maintain an erection—she had playfully yanked the cap off Matt's head. Before Matt could stop her, she'd flung his Eagles cap across the room.

"Mr. Wheeler wants to get a grub, too!" Onika announced.

Completely perplexed, both Matt and Puddin stared at Onika.

"Mr. Wheeler got the hots for you," Onika explained.

I do not! Matt shouted in his mind. But he knew better than to contradict Onika out loud.

"He was checking out your big ass when you got out of the van."

Puddin blushed. "Get outta here. You lying?"

"I'm not lying. Mr. Wheeler wants to eat your pussy. Don't you, boo." Teasingly, Onika elbowed Matt, causing the hand that shielded his personals to slip away. Horrified at Onika's suggestion, Matt was too stunned to speak and too shocked to care about his penis.

"Dayum! Where's the rest of his dick?" Puddin' blurted and then cracked up in laughter. Red-faced with embarrassment, Matt immediately clamped both hands over his penis.

"It's small right now, but it'll grow a couple more inches when it gets hard. But you ain't gotta worry about him trying to use it. He don't wanna fuck nobody but me. I gotta make a quick run. I need you to feed him some pussy so he can stay hard 'til I get back."

Puddin giggled. "Y'all crazy, but aiight. I'll do it. You know me, I ain't never turned down no food or no opportunity to get my pussy ate," Puddin replied with a big, cheesy grin. She clenched the sandwich between her teeth as she unhooked the chain that dangled through the loops of her jeans.

Puddin looked so disgusting with the sandwich hanging out of her mouth that Matt felt compelled to put his foot down and stand up to Onika. "Onika!" he said firmly, "What the hell is wrong with you. I'm not—"

Before Matt could utter another word, Onika drew her hand back and sent a stinging slap across his face. His hands went to his face, defensively.

"See what I mean, Puddin?" Onika remarked, attempting to explain her violent response. "Do you see how I gotta keep him in check?" Breathing hard, Onika shook her head. "Dealing with this nigga is hard work."

"I can see that," Puddin agreed sympathetically. Neglecting to finish peeling off the too-tight jeans, she once again attacked the ham and cheese sandwich, while watching in fascination as Matt's small dick quivered and sprang to life.

Onika smiled down at her accomplishment. "Tough love! That's all my boo needs," Onika bragged. She scowled at Puddin. "Damn, girl. Hurry up and get outta those jeans. You gotta squat over Mr. Wheeler and keep him occupied while I make my run."

"I'm moving as fast as I can. But I'm a big girl—it takes me a minute to struggle out of my clothes."

Finally stripped naked, Puddin maneuvered over and straddled

Matt's face and pressed her pussy against his unwilling mouth while she munched happily on her swiftly dwindling sandwich.

Allowing himself to be debased by Onika and her fat friend was disgusting and arousing at the same time, and he felt his penis stiffen. It was hard enough to slip inside Onika. He was sure of it. But Onika, dressing quickly, had other plans.

"Suck her pussy real good, boo," Onika said with affection as she strolled out of the bedroom.

With Onika's blessings, Puddin enthusiastically rotated her pussy against Matt's unwilling lips. Mayonnaise dripped from her sandwich, dotting Matt's forehead as well as the air mattress he lay upon.

CHAPTER 15

Waiting around for Mr. Wheeler to show up had Cochise fuming mad. He had no way of contacting his boss. Cochise was furious with himself also. The boss's business card with his cell phone number printed at the bottom was tucked inside a drawer in his room at the Recovery House. Shit! He'd never thought to carry the card to work with him. Why would he, when there had never been any reason to contact Mr. Wheeler? The boss was always Johnny-on-the-spot when it came to picking up the crew.

Cochise stared upward as if the answer to his dilemma was emblazoned on the ceiling. Suddenly, his mind's eye recalled opening a box that contained a dozen bottles of cleaning solution. His wandering mind also recalled seeing a label of sort on the side of the box. Cochise hurried over to the reception desk where he'd stacked the supplies and equipment. He quickly located the box and sure enough, a printed label with Mr. Wheeler's home address was glued to the side of the box.

Digging in his pockets for bus fare, Cochise exited the office building. He looked back at the unlocked door and shrugged. He didn't have any keys to lock the door, so fuck it. Mr. Wheeler deserved to get his equipment jacked.

Cochise got off the bus on Greene Street and walked the few blocks to his boss's house. Tulpehocken Street was peaceful, tree-lined with well-maintained homes. Instead of ringing the doorbell, Cochise walked to the end of the block and rounded the corner that led to the back of Mr. Wheeler's home. There was a shiny Buick LaCrosse in the driveway, which Cochise figured belonged to the boss's wife. But Mr. Wheeler's van was nowhere to be found. The slimy bastard was still in Chester, still getting it on with Onika. Well, Cochise didn't have all night to lurk in the shadows like a crackhead waiting for his dealer. Taking long, purposeful strides, he walked back around the block and stepped up to his boss's front door.

Though Cochise didn't have a plan, he boldly rang the doorbell.

He heard movement and knew the boss's wife was looking at him through the peephole. "Who is it?" she asked. Her tone sounded more curious than annoyed.

"I'm sorry to disturb you, ma'am, but, uh, I work for your husband. There was a problem at the job. I don't have the number to your husband's cell and I was wondering if you'd call him—"

The door opened. A pretty, honey-complexioned woman stood in the doorway.

Most women would be afraid to welcome a six-foot-six stranger into their home, so Cochise relaxed his facial muscles, intending to look as harmless and non-threatening as possible. "My name's Langston Belgrave, everybody calls me Cochise," he said, smiling. His smile, he hoped, conveyed that he came in peace.

Mrs. Wheeler gave a quick smile as she stepped aside. "Come in, Cochise. Matt has mentioned your name. Did something happen to him?" Her voice trembled with worry.

"No, ma'am, nothing happened to Mr. Wheeler. I'm sure he's all right. He said he had some business to take care of..."

"I'm Regina Wheeler, Matt's wife," the attractive woman said, anxiously raking her hand through curls held together by a hair clip. "What kind of business did Matt have to take care of this time of night?" Regina queried politely.

"I don't know what your husband had to do. He doesn't tell the workers, uh, his personal business." Mr. Wheeler's wife seemed upset and Cochise didn't see any reason to tell her that he strongly suspected that her husband was out knocking boots with a much younger chick. "One of the men got sick on the job and like I said, I don't have your husband's cell phone number on me. Would you mind giving him a call?" Cochise wasn't trying to get Mr. Wheeler busted or anything, but it was critical that he and the men get paid.

"Sure," Regina said, picking up the phone. She pushed a number and then frowned. "It's ringing," she said, "but he's not picking up." She disconnected the call and then pushed ten digits instead of using speed dial. Confused, she shook her head. "Now I'm getting his voicemail."

Cochise shrugged uncomfortably.

"Matt, call home as soon as you get this message," Regina spoke into the phone. Looking concerned, she turned her attention back to Cochise. "That's odd. Matt never turns his phone off when he's away from home. Do you think I should call the police?" Her face was etched with worry.

Cochise knew Mr. Wheeler was just fine and he had a pretty good idea why the scumbag had turned his cell off, but blowing the whistle on his boss's indiscretions wasn't the reason for the visit.

"Mrs. Wheeler," Cochise said softly, "I'm sure your husband's okay. He told us the meeting might take a long time. He told us to just chill at the building we were cleaning until he got back," Cochise lied, trying to set Mrs. Wheeler's mind at ease. "Mr. Faison got sick and I thought it was best for Theo to take him back to Chester." Cochise was relieved that that part of the story was true. He hated lying to the lady. "The problem is we haven't been paid and, um..." Damn, he hadn't planned on having to tell his troubles to the boss's wife. It was embarrassing. He felt like kicking Mr. Wheeler's ass for getting him into this predicament. Here he was, fumbling with his words, looking like a nut in front of the man's pretty wife.

And speaking of pretty, how the hell did corny-ass Mr. Wheeler luck up on such a good-looking wife? The man had to be crazy to cheat on her for that smut Onika.

Mrs. Wheeler was wearing an ankle-length robe of a soft fabric. Absently, she tightened the sash, pulling the soft fabric snugly around her body, revealing a slim waistline and nicely rounded hips. Sexually starved, Cochise felt a sudden rush of heat that settled in his groin. He hadn't checked out a woman in a sexual way since he'd broken up with Shawna and he hadn't meant to look at the boss's wife in that way. But his dick, with a mind of its own, woke up and started stirring to life.

Pulling his eyes from the danger zone of her hips, he directed his attention to the floor, but the visual below was equally risky. A silver toe ring glimmered from one of Mrs. Wheeler's pretty, slender feet. Damn, he was really hard up, getting turned on by a toe ring and a pair of feet!

Cochise could have used a hat or something to place in front of his crotch. His dick was acting up something terrible, jerking and twitching without even a semblance of self control. If he didn't do something about his problem, a wet spot would soon appear on the front of his pants. With his jawn swelling up and threatening to burst through the heavy-duty fabric of his work pants, Cochise felt uncomfortable and uneasy. If this lady caught a glimpse of his big dick trying to poke a hole through his pants, she was liable to think he was plotting on rape. Who could blame her if she panicked and called the cops?

"Do you mind if I sit down?" Cochise asked humbly.

"No, I don't mind. Excuse my manners, please have a seat." She waved her hand in the direction of a tan leather sofa.

Cochise sat down on the sofa, hoping that a seated position would take some of the pressure off his manhood. "So, um, like I was saying…Mr. Wheeler told us he left our pay vouchers home. If my man wasn't all sick and everything, I wouldn't be here acting all pressed," Cochise explained awkwardly.

"I hear what you're saying, but I honestly don't know where Matt keeps the pay vouchers. I can look in his office, but I doubt—"

Frustrated, Cochise interrupted. "I'd appreciate it if you'd take a look."

Regina nodded. A few minutes later, she glided back into the living room, waving three slips of paper. "They were on top of his desk, right in plain sight," she said with a smile. She was even prettier when she smiled, Cochise noted. *I gotta stop this. My ass is buggin'; this shit ain't cool at all.*

When his dick finally calmed down, Cochise stood up. Keeping his eyes focused anywhere but on Mrs. Wheeler, Cochise waited for her to give him the vouchers.

"This is odd," Regina said as she scanned each voucher. "Doesn't Matt employ three men and a young lady from the womens' Recovery House?"

Cochise nodded. "Yeah, Onika. I don't know. Maybe he keeps her voucher separate." Cochise sighed. "I don't know what's up with her; she didn't come to work today."

Regina scowled slightly. "I hope the young lady didn't relapse."

She probably is, he wanted to say. "I don't know," he said, shrugging his shoulders and averting his gaze.

When Regina handed Cochise the vouchers, their hands touched briefly. The moment their flesh touched, Cochise felt something similar to an electrical jolt. Their eyes met and locked. Though Regina kept her cool, Cochise was certain she'd felt the strong connection, too.

Something important had just gone down, but what could he do about it? Scoop her up in his arms, ask her to leave her husband and her lovely home and run away with him to...where? His cramped, sparsely furnished room? *Yeah, right. Keep dreamin'.* Cochise laughed to himself as he pocketed the pay vouchers.

"Thanks again," he told Regina Wheeler. "When you hear from your husband, let him know that he needs to lock up the spot where we were working."

"I'll be sure I tell him," Regina said. The spark he'd seen in her eyes earlier was gone. She looked distracted as she walked Cochise to the door.

"Good night. Uh, don't worry, I'm sure Mr. Wheeler is all right."

Regina nodded. "I hope so. Good night, Cochise."

CHAPTER 16

Onika parked Matt's van outside the house on Third Street and rounded the corner to Ward Street. Just in case Mr. Wheeler had found a way to follow her, she looked over her shoulder as she hurried down the street. She stopped in front of a house with a board covering one of the windows. There wasn't a doorbell or a knocker on the old, splintered, wooden front door. "Yo, it's Onika," she yelled as she kicked the door.

After a minute or so, Onika was admitted inside the squalid crackhouse. "'What's good, Onika," greeted a grinning eighteen-year-old hustler named Nazier who worked around the clock but turned most of his earnings over to the dealer who fronted him product. Nazier was dressed in black sweat pants and a matching hoodie. He wore black to camouflage the dirt that accumulated on his clothes after sitting inside the filthy home for two or three days at a time while he collected money from the addicts who streamed through twenty-four hours a day.

"Ain't shit, young buck," Onika replied as she slid Nazier forty dollars to join the drug party.

"I ain't sharing shit," she informed the group of dull-eyed addicts whose faces had lit up with expectancy when she arrived on the set. Onika examined the product. "This shit better be good," she told Nazier gruffly.

And it was. She greedily sucked in fumes and quickly depleted her funds.

"Lemme hold something. I'll get back with you tomorrow, aiight?" Onika asked Nazier. Her tone was now soft and flirty.

"I ain't frontin' you nuffin tonight," Nazier told her. "I'm dealing with cash money only, baby."

"Stop playin', Naz. Lemme hold something," she insisted, her voice rising.

"Whassup, money?" yelled an impatient male customer, holding up an empty pipe.

"I gotchu, my man," Nazier replied and then turned his attention back to Onika. "Aiight, go upstairs. I'll be up after I take care of my man over here." Nazier bent at the waist, unzipped a hidden pocket at the bottom of his sweats, and retrieved two small plastic bags.

"Hurry up," Onika snapped with renewed sass. With her eyes fastened hungrily on the product Nazier held in the palm of his hand, Onika moved slowly up the stairs.

"Go 'head, man," Nazier told Onika. "Give me a minute. I said I'ma get witchu!"

Reluctantly, Onika climbed the stairs. There were three bedrooms, two were locked. Besides the open door to the bathroom, which was without running water, the only other open door led to a room with tattered bath towels nailed to the windows.

Inside the bedroom, Onika was hit with a nauseating stench. A skinny, malnourished cat lounged on rags in a corner and a plastic container that was filled with more feces than kitty litter sat nearby. Clothing-filled trash bags were strewn about and large boxes that served as dresser drawers were piled up all over the room. A box spring and soiled bare mattress were the only furnishings inside the squalid bedroom. Onika turned up her nose and disgustedly left the room. At that moment, Nazier bounded the stairs.

"Whaddup?"

"We gotta make this quick. Two bags for some head," she said, standing in the hallway.

"Man, I don't need no blowjob," Nazier informed her, frowning. "I just got my dick wet before you came through." Nazier grabbed Onika's hand and crudely pressed it against his length. "My shit is hard as granite. I'm ready to bust inside some pussy."

"Aiight, but make it quick," Onika said and quickly pulled off her jeans. Not wanting her clothing to make contact with the grimy wooden floor, she threw her jeans over her shoulder and then braced herself against a wall.

Nazier gawked at Onika. "You kidding? You want me to knock it out while I'm standing up?"

"Yeah, why not?" Onika caressed her mons, trying to entice him.

A wry smile touched his lips. "Man, fuck you. I ain't wit dat dumb shit." Nazier turned toward the stairs.

"Okay. Damn! You get on my nerves, Naz." Onika straightened her shoulders as she forced herself to enter the foul-smelling bedroom.

She positioned her jeans and stretchy top on the stained mattress, using them as a barrier between her naked buttocks and the soiled mattress.

Holding Onika's thighs wide apart, Nazier entered her. His dick strokes were gentle at first, but his pace soon quickened to a pounding tempo. He hammered her semi-moist pussy without the least bit of concern for the discomfort he was causing.

The malnourished cat wandered over and climbed on the mattress. Onika, uncomfortable and angry, swung a tightly balled fist at the cat, sending it skidding across the room. She glared at the cat and then turned a hard look at Nazier. "Damn, Naz. Whatchu waiting for? Hurry up and bust. You said we was gon' take care of some business."

"Whatchu think I'm doing," he snarled, pumping dick without mercy.

"I'm talking about the rocks you promised to give me," she said between painful gasps.

"Yeah, I'm talking about rocks, too." He gave a malicious chuckle. "I probably could get my rocks off if you would shut the fuck up." Nazier embedded his dick and then yanked it out, viciously. "I like to take my time when I'm fucking," he explained as he repeated the process.

"That shit hurts. You acting like you gon' keep this up for hours. Hmph! You crazy if you think I'm gon' just lay here and let you bang out my pussy." Onika lifted herself up and rested on her elbows. "If you're having trouble getting off, you need to pull your dick out and let me suck on it."

Nazier slowed down and then came to a stop. Looking down at Onika, he said, "Aiight, I'm gon' let you get on it for a minute, to cool it off. It feels like your dry-ass pussy is burnin' the skin off my jawn."

"Fuck you, Naz." She rolled her eyes.

"Yeah, whatever," he muttered. "But when I'm ready to bust, though, you gotta lay your ass back down and spread your legs." He tightened his grip on his steely manhood, aiming it at Onika, threateningly. "Big boy," he said, referring to his penis, "don't like to waste no seed. He wanna be deep up in that pussy hole when he's ready to bust."

Onika nodded. She got on her knees, prepared to guzzle

Nazier's dick with enthusiasm and passion, giving him no choice but to quickly ejaculate. Her plan was delayed by her ringing cell phone. "Hold up," she told Nazier, pulling the phone out of the back pocket of her jeans. She frowned at the screen, put it on vibrate, and tossed it on the mattress next to her clothes. *Mr. Wheeler had better leave me the fuck alone while I'm handling my business.*

A few moments later, Nazier groaned and yanked his dick out of Onika's mouth. He pushed her onto her back and roughly drove his saliva-slick dick into her aching vagina, quickly filling it with semen.

Nazier got up and adjusted his clothes and then turned his back to Onika. He unzipped yet another secret pocket in his baggy sweatpants, then turned and faced Onika. "I ain't giving out no more freebies tonight," Nazier warned. Onika sucked her teeth, snatched up the plastic bags, dressed hurriedly and then rushed downstairs to rejoin the party.

Running out of supply, Nazier left the crackhouse for about a half hour. When he returned Onika could see the bulging pockets that were filled with miniature plastic bags containing the object of her desire. Sexily, Onika sidled up to Nazier again.

Nazier looked at her with contempt. "Man, you got to come at me with a better offer. I ain't feeling you like that right now."

She presented her new cell phone.

"Fuck outta here. I got about twenty phones," Nazier barked. "You gon' have to step up your game."

"Oh, my game is tight," Onika bragged. "I got my whip parked around the corner on Third Street. But you gon' have to come out of pocket if you want to rent my ride."

"You pushin' something fly?"

"Nah, just something to get around in." She described Matt's van. Nazier didn't look impressed. "Well, fuck it. It's more than you got. You ain't pushin' shit," she reminded him. "Look, my van is sturdy and I just filled the tank. That's a helluva deal."

Nazier nodded in agreement. "I can dig it. So, how long you gon' let me hold it for?"

"Couple hours," Onika offered.

Nazier tossed her four bags and Onika tossed him the keys to Matt's van.

When her drugs ran out, Onika auctioned off her cell phone to the highest bidder. Someone waved a ten-dollar-bill, and Onika quickly snatched it.

Finally tapped out and possessing nothing else to sell, Onika felt angry at the world. Exhausted and hungry, she was ready to leave the drug den, but Nazier hadn't returned with the van.

Tired of waiting, she left the house, walked a half block, and flagged down a cab.

CHAPTER 17

Ordered by Onika to sex Puddin with his tongue, Matt had never felt so victimized or helpless in his life. Puddin had to be the most disgusting person he'd ever come into such intimate contact with. While straddling him, not only did the slovenly young woman dribble mayonnaise on Matt's head and face, but she practically smothered him with the heft of her body. Disgust coursed through him, yet oddly, Matt felt his sluggish penis spring to life. Lapping Puddin's juices, Matt closed his hand tightly around the base of his rigid shaft to prevent himself from ejaculating too quickly.

"Oops!" Puddin exclaimed as a sudden burst of air was loudly expelled from her vagina into Matt's open mouth. "My bad," she apologized, but continued gyrating on his face. "Ain't nothing but a pussy pop," she casually explained. "You was workin' that tongue so good, you had my pussy bubbling up and popping and carrying on."

Repelled, Matt bolted up, toppling Puddin off of him. Momentarily stunned, she lay flat on her back, arms splayed out on top of the air mattress. Matt couldn't help but notice her heavy breasts and hard pink nipples that jutted outward. Inexplicably, revulsion turned to sexual desire.

There was no mistaking the lust in Matt's eyes. Puddin's eyes shot down to his rising penis. Excited by Matt's arousal, Puddin drew up her knees and slowly parted her fleshy thighs, flashing a pair of fat, pink pussy lips. "You wanna sex a big girl, Mr. Wheeler?"

Matt consented with a grunt. Puddin pulled him on top of her and guided his small shaft into her soggy entrance. Incredibly, Matt stroked Puddin for ten minutes before his dick went soft.

"Sit on my face," he whispered urgently.

Without hesitation, Puddin straddled him.

"Can you do that thing again?" His perverted request embarrassed him, but he was desperate for assistance.

"You want me to shoot off some more pussy farts?" Puddin asked, surprised.

In his normal mindset, Matt would not be aroused by a gross bodily function, but Matt was not working with a rational mind when he opened his mouth wide, nodding his head in consent.

Puddin lifted up slightly, arched her back, and sucked air into her vaginal canal.

Amazingly, Matt was able to maintain an erection with Puddin. Though she possessed neither Onika's bossy nature nor her predisposition to violence, there was something about her that made him rigid with desire. He supposed it was her big bosom and her crude behavior that kept his dick hard, motivating him to fuck her five times in a row.

But that was hours ago and the pride he'd felt at his ability to perform like a young stud had dissipated. At present, Matt was worried sick about his van and pissed at himself, Onika, and Puddin.

Puddin, oblivious to Matt's anger and stress, was sprawled out on the air mattress, sound asleep and snoring loudly. The smell of sex permeated the bedroom.

Though Matt felt that he'd done an admirable job of fucking Puddin's brains out, he honestly couldn't take credit for her being stretched out and dead to the world. She was in an Oxy stupor, which was fine with Matt. He would not have enjoyed being forced to make polite after-sex chit-chat after participating in such vulgarities with someone he found beneath contempt.

Matt paced frantically back and forth from the kitchen to the living room. Every ten minutes or so, overwrought with anxiety, he'd slump down into the paint-splattered metal chair. Each time he heard the sound of tires rolling into the parking lot, he'd spring from the chair, and rush to the window, and peek through the blinds. Disappointment would escalate to rage, and as he again dialed Onika's cell phone number, he would push the buttons with such force, he was surprised his phone didn't shatter.

Matt had already left a series of angry, urgent messages, but after another half hour had passed without hearing from her, Matt became so incensed he flipped open his phone again, this time intending to leave Onika a profanity-laced message. At that moment, his phone rang. His heart lifted in relief. But seeing his home number on the screen, he quickly turned off the phone and snapped it shut. He couldn't deal with his wife. Not right now. He'd return her call when he'd retrieved his van and was headed toward Philly.

How had he allowed Onika to get him into such a tight spot? What had he been thinking when he turned over the keys to his van to the reckless young girl? Filled with self disgust, Matt had to admit that he'd been thinking with the wrong head.

His crew was stranded at the job and if he didn't remedy the disastrous situation quickly, he could lose the contract he had with the Recovery House. Hell, he could lose his business if something happened to one of the men while left unsupervised. Imagining the worst-case scenario, Matt envisioned himself being hit with a lawsuit and losing everything he owned trying to pay off legal fees. Feeling a bad headache coming on, he removed his Eagles cap and anxiously rubbed his forehead.

Suddenly, Matt heard the jangle of keys. With great relief, he jumped up and hurried to the living room.

"Mr. Wheeler!" Onika shouted as she burst through the door. "You ain't gon' believe this shit."

Matt gawked at her. Terror gripped his heart.

"Your van got jacked!"

Matt's stomach dropped. His frantic eyes searched Onika's face for a sign that she was playing a prank.

"Some doped-up young buck held a gun right up to the window. When he told me to give up the whip, I did what he said. I wasn't tryin' to argue with a nut aiming a gun in my face. Feel me?" she added, dashing Matt's hopes that she was joking.

Looking grim, Matt flipped open his cell. "I have to call the police."

"Wait a minute, Mr. Wheeler. We gotta get our story together before you drag the cops into this mess."

"Are you crazy! I'm not fabricating a story. I have to get my van back. Tonight!"

"It ain't like the cops are gon' rush out and search for your van. They just gon' make you file a report."

"Then I'll file a report!" Matt retorted.

"Yeah, but you'll make out better if we go out and search for it. I think I know where it is."

"You do?" Matt exclaimed, marveling at the absurdity of the situation.

"Uh-huh. The young buck who jacked it probably sold it to this drug dealer named Naz. I know where Naz sets up shop. Grab your coat, Mr. Wheeler; I got a cab waiting for us in the parking lot."

This was a matter for the police. But, too desperate to listen to the warning alarms that went off in his head, and against his better judgment, Matt followed Onika out the door.

Onika sat up front with the driver while Matt situated himself in the rear.

"Take us to Third and Ward," she told the driver. The driver twisted around and took a look at Matt and then turned to Onika. "You owe me seven dollars. I'm not moving this cab until you pay."

Onika sucked her teeth. "Ain't nobody trying to rob you." She looked over her shoulder at Matt. "Give this nut the cab fare, Mr. Wheeler."

"I'm not a nut," the cab driver said, sharpening his tone. "You're very disrespectful. And why do you insist on sitting up front when I already told you it's against regulations?"

Onika flipped her hand at the driver and turned to Matt. "You got the money?"

The situation was progressing from bad to worse. Helplessly, Matt groped in his pants pocket and extracted a ten.

"Lemme hold your phone for a second, Mr. Wheeler. I need to call one of my peoples to see if anybody knows anything about your van."

Too distraught to even wonder why she didn't make the call with her own phone, Matt listlessly handed Onika his phone. As luck would have it, Matt's phone rang the minute it touched Onika's hand. And Onika answered it as if the phone were her very own.

"Some lady—your wife, I guess—wants to speak to you," Onika nonchalantly told Matt. "Here you go, boo," she said, handing the phone to Matt.

Waving both hands and shaking his head in terror, Matt refused to speak with his wife.

Onika repositioned the phone next to her ear. "Yo, we 'bout to get into something right now. He said he'll call you back," Onika told Regina and then disconnected the call.

"Why'd you have to open your mouth? Why didn't you just hang up?" Matt yelled at Onika.

"Oh, now you wanna put that bitch in front of me! Fuck it, then. After we get your van back, you ain't gotta worry about me no more."

Slouched in the backseat and deeply troubled, Matt tried to process the distressful situation. Before hooking up with Onika, he'd never cheated on his wife. He'd place his hand on a stack of Bibles and testify that his involvement with the rough, young girl was totally out of character; he'd been temporary insane.

And it wasn't his fault. Regina had been hounding him, telling him he needed to see a doctor, urging him to get medical help for his sexual dysfunction. It was a low blow to be told by your wife that you couldn't satisfy her needs.

Before Regina started complaining, he hadn't paid Onika any attention. He was feeling less than a man when Onika first came on to him. When he couldn't perform, she coerced him into giving her oral sex and that one taste turned out to be the magical elixir that solved his problem. In his heart, he hadn't been trying to hurt Regina, he was simply trying to prove to himself that he was a real man. After tonight, he fully intended to leave Onika alone. He'd kick her out of the apartment and then try to figure out a way to break the lease without too much damage to his pockets.

Regina! It pained him to think of her going through the phone book, searching for a divorce attorney. Matt shot daggers at the back of Onika's head. Why'd she have to answer his phone? Onika had caused some major damage in his marriage and it would take a miracle to keep Regina from filing for divorce.

The cab stopped in front of a house on Ward Street, and Matt could hardly believe his eyes. Parked at the curb was his van! "There it is!" Matt shouted.

"Fall back, Mr. Wheeler. You better let me handle this. You don't know nothin' about the streets. I might have to bargain with Naz. How much cash can you come up with? Naz ain't gon' give you your van back for free."

"You sound like a lunatic. I'm not intimidated by some street thug!" Matt jumped out of the cab and rushed toward the driver's side of his van.

"Yo, dude. What's your problem?" Nazier snapped in surprise when Matt suddenly yanked the door open.

"This is my van, get the hell out!" Matt demanded, too indignant to fear the hardened younger man who was sitting in the driver's seat of his van.

"Aiight, money. But you ain't gotta come at me like that. You lucky I ain't pull out my burner."

"Get out of my van!" Seething, Matt spoke through clenched teeth.

"Aiight, aiight." Lazily, Nazier leaned over and reached for the handle to the glove compartment.

Matt grabbed Nazier's shirttail and yanked hard, forcing the young man's fingers to slip off the handle. "Who do you think you are, rifling through my glove compartment? Get out!" Matt was amazed at the audacity of the young punk.

Nazier twisted around. "Get the fuck off me," he yelled as he fired a series of punches to Matt's face and head.

Stunned as he was by the unexpected, powerful blows, it took Matt a moment to comprehend what was happening. Then he fought back, swinging wildly, but doing no damage to the young hoodlum. Frustrated, Matt used all the strength he could muster and yanked Nazier out of the van. With Matt still holding on to Nazier's shirt, the two scuffled until Matt mustered the strength to shove the drug dealer to the ground.

With his opponent momentarily down, Matt swiftly jumped into the driver's seat, slammed the door shut, and locked it. As Matt revved the engine, Nazier scrambled to his feet, pointing fiercely and shouting epithets. Matt shot out of the parking spot and floored the accelerator.

To hell with Onika and everyone associated with her. Speeding through the streets of Chester, Matt vowed to cancel the furniture delivery, evict Onika from the apartment, and never stray from home again. Somehow, he'd patch things up with him and Regina. Resuming a normal life with his wife would be heaven after the harrowing hell he'd experienced with Onika.

Still speeding as he practiced the speech he'd give Regina, he was suddenly blinded by an array of flashing lights that filled his rearview mirror. The police. *Damn, damn, damn!* Matt pulled over, his brain in overdrive as he tried to figure out how to talk his way out of a speeding ticket.

The police officer approached the van. Matt slid down the window. "Is there a problem?" he asked, grinning sheepishly.

"License, registration, and insurance identification," the officer said dryly.

"Sure thing," Matt said cheerily. He pulled open the glove compartment. His eyes widened in sheer disbelief. A gun lay next to a quart-sized, sealed plastic bag filled with what appeared to be a couple dozen small packs of crack. His heart dropped to his stomach. Time seemed suspended.

"Hands up!" the cop bellowed. With his hands up and trembling, Matt turned toward the officer.

"It's not mine! I swear—" His mouth clamped shut as he gazed inside the barrel of the officer's gun. One false move, a jerky, nervous reaction, and Matt knew he could instantly become a statistic, the victim of a trigger-happy cop, shot in self-defense for reaching for a loaded weapon. So Matt sat perfectly still, kept his hands where they could be seen, and waited for permission to speak. He was certain that after he told the cop about the harrowing evening he'd had, how he was forced to hunt down his stolen van, and had to resort to fist-fighting with a young thug to get the van back, after he explained to the cop that he was a law-abiding citizen with a business to run, there was no way he'd be detained on the side of the road for very long.

CHAPTER 18

Waiting at the bus stop, Cochise checked the time. One o'clock in the morning. Damn! A few motorists whizzed by. A box-shaped truck made its late-night run, but there wasn't a bus in sight. The temperature had dropped since he'd left the job site; he stuck his cold hands in his jacket pockets to warm them and stepped out to the curb, again.

A half hour later, the bus still hadn't arrived. Being that he was the only person standing at the bus stop, he couldn't help but wonder if maybe he'd missed the last bus. He didn't have a bus schedule and didn't know much about the public transportation system in Philly, but there was a grim possibility that he was standing around waiting in vain. *Shit!*

Cochise figured Mr. Wheeler had gotten home by now. His cheatin' ass was probably snuggled up next to his unsuspecting, sexy wife right now. Craning his neck, he looked for the bright headlights of the bus one last time. Still no luck. *Fuck this!* Feeling righteously indignant and getting angrier by the minute, Cochise turned around and headed back to Mr. Wheeler's house. The boss was going to have to drag his ass out of bed and take Cochise the fuck back to Chester.

When Mrs. Wheeler opened the door, Cochise was stunned by the drastic change in her appearance. Her face looked swollen, her eyes were bloodshot. Holding a handful of tissues, she dabbed at falling tears.

Cochise gawked at the boss's wife, bewildered. "What's wrong?" He stepped inside, his brow knitted in concern as he gently closed the door.

"I called Matt's cell after you left," she said between sobs.

"Is he all right?"

"I guess," Regina said quietly. "A woman answered his phone. An obnoxious young woman who referred to *my* husband as boo. She didn't come right out and say it, but she hinted that she and Matt were having sex." Regina gasped in anguish and visibly shuddered at the memory. "That woman who answered Matt's phone was so crude and disrespectful, I just can't imagine Matt getting involved with someone like that." Regina shook her head emphatically. "How could I have been so blind, thinking Matt was putting in extra hours at work while he was involved in a lurid affair?"

Cochise shook his head sympathetically. The boss and Onika had been kicking it for quite a while. It was only a matter of time before Mr. Wheeler got busted. Only God knew what had provoked the man to put his marriage on the line for someone as hardcore, gangly, and unattractive as Onika. Imagining the harsh words that Onika had hurled at Mrs. Wheeler, Cochise's expression grew somber. It was a shame for such a nice lady to be disrespected that way.

"Somebody could have been playing around with his phone. You never know," Cochise suggested, attempting to lessen Mrs.

Wheeler's pain. "Did your husband call you back…you know, to explain what happened?"

"No. He turned his phone off," Regina said bitterly. A scowl formed on her face. Her eyelashes fluttered rapidly as she struggled to blink back a fresh batch of tears. Then, giving in to wracking sobs, she fell against Cochise.

Reflexively, Cochise opened his arms, held her. He patted Regina's back and rubbed in circular motions as she sobbed against his broad chest. He didn't know what to say, but felt he should say something encouraging. "It's all right. Don't cry," he muttered awkwardly. Regina cried harder. Cochise tightened his arms around her. He rocked her and found himself offering murmurs of consolation, soothing utterances that weren't quite words. When her crying subsided, she mopped her tears with the back of her hand. But sensing there were more tears yet to fall, Cochise led Regina to the sofa and gently lowered her. In a seated position, he comforted his boss's pretty wife, enveloping her in his massive arms. With her face buried in his shirt, Regina sobbed. Cochise stroked her dark hair, a helmet of curls that had fallen free from the hair clip. He sensed her loneliness, the layers of once-deep sorrow now so close to the surface he could feel her pain as keenly as he felt his own.

When her sniffling subsided, Regina grew quiet and still. Then she raised her head and Cochise saw the hurt in her eyes; he saw the reflection of his own pained expression and in an instant felt an even deeper connection with Regina Wheeler.

And there was something else. Was she attracted to him? By the time Cochise recognized the raw desire that shone in Regina's eyes, she had slipped out of her robe. A silk gown clung to her body. Wordlessly, she gazed at him, then cupped his face and pressed her mouth against his.

Taken off guard by the sweetness of her lips, by the rush of heat that engorged his loins, Cochise had difficulty processing what was taking place. Seconds later, the initial shock subsided and his lips relaxed against hers. The purpose of his visit—to get a ride back to Chester—seemed totally unimportant as his tongue slowly penetrated Regina's lips and caressed her tongue until she shivered in his arms.

Becoming lost inside the kiss, he forced himself to pull away. *This is crazy*, Cochise thought as he searched her face for a sign that they'd gone too far. Her eyes told him she wanted more.

Regina Wheeler had never seduced anyone in her life; had never initiated a sexual liaison. Perhaps she wouldn't have behaved so boldly had she not noticed the way Cochise's eyes had swept over her body earlier that evening. She'd felt both self-conscious and flattered that the much younger man had taken notice and found her appealing.

Cochise was a hottie. His striking good looks had both startled and enticed her, but she would have never imagined that an hour or so later she'd be shamelessly seducing him, kissing him with a fiery passion.

Cochise was a stunning, muscular, towering figure with erotic long, dark hair. He was an irresistible magnet for Regina's pent-up sexual desire. Giving in to demanding carnal urges, Regina tugged at the sleeve of Cochise's jacket, coaxing him to come out of it. A fire raged between her legs and she yearned for the beautiful stranger to extinguish the flames.

His strong hands wandered over the satin-covered contours of her body, her breasts, her stomach, and full hips and thighs. He stroked her thighs, his hand gliding upward.

Ripe with need, Regina opened her legs.

"Mrs. Wheeler. I don't want you to do something you'll regret…"

"I want you," she whispered helplessly.

Demonstrating that he wanted her, too, Cochise drew Regina into a tight embrace.

Needing to feel his lips on her flesh, she pulled the thin straps of her gown off her shoulders, freeing her breasts. Alternately, Cochise kissed each perfectly formed breast, capturing the nipples between his teeth and flicking his tongue against the aroused buds, and then moved to her neck, nibbling at her flesh, making her moan, causing her to tangle her fingers in his mass of long hair.

Regina slid her hands beneath his shirt, exploring what felt like miles of concrete muscles. "Take off your clothes," she said in a breathy voice she barely recognized as her own.

Cochise raised his shirt over his head, revealing the hard muscles that rippled beneath his hot flesh. Unable to resist touching him, Regina cupped a hand over a concrete bicep and then moved upward to his strong shoulders. Tenderly, she moved her hand across the solid wall of steel that was his chest. Seeing and touching the expanse of his large manly form aroused her and nearly took her breath away.

Cochise reached for her; he placed a trail of kisses from her neck down to her stomach. Regina moaned in helpless surrender. But Cochise did not move toward her pleasure center. Urgently, Regina sought Cochise's hand and guided it to the furnace that raged between her legs. An agonized gasp escaped her lips the moment his fingers brushed against her most sensitive place.

Skillful fingers separated her dewy petals. Regina cried out in ecstasy. Involuntarily her hips rose, her legs parted eagerly. Cochise inserted his longest finger into her flaming hot spot. He worked his finger, moving it in and out slowly, giving Regina pleasure so intense, she cried out his name.

Taking in short, heated breaths, Regina rocked her hips in a desperate rhythm.

"You want me, baby?" Cochise asked in a husky voice as he probed deeply inside her smoldering secret place.

"Yes. I want to feel—" Her words were cut off by body shivers and ragged gasps as Cochise's long finger undulated inside, stroking her walls, giving her waves of pleasure that threatened to take her over the edge. "I want to feel you inside me. Take these off," she pleaded, pulling at the belt that encircled Cochise's tapered waist.

Instead of taking off his pants, Cochise embraced Regina and whispered in her ear. "I dig you, you know?"

She nodded.

"I don't want to hurt you and I don't want to disrespect your home."

"Matt already disrespected our home," Regina responded, defending the daring act of passion that was taking place. A part of her wanted to hurt her husband as he'd hurt her. But another, deeper part of her spirit didn't care about exacting revenge. Admittedly, Regina felt a burning desire to be sexually fulfilled. But there was also a great need to be in a relationship where she was valued. Cherished. Loved. For some idiotic reason, she believed with all her heart that it was possible to have all of that with Cochise. But how could she explain that to this man she barely knew? A man who didn't even refer to her by her first name?

"The way I see it," Cochise continued, eyeing her intently,

"you're mad at your husband and you want to get even with him for what he did to you. But I'm really feelin' you, Mrs. Wheeler. My emotions are on the line," Cochise admitted, touching his chest sincerely.

"Regina. Call me Regina." She took a breath, prepared to confess that she was completely captivated, but the blaring ring of the phone put her words on pause. She turned sharply toward the sound. "It's Matt, I know it," she said quietly. With a sigh, she rose and crossed the room.

CHAPTER 19

"Regina! I'm locked up!" Matt blurted out when Regina picked up the cordless. "There's been a terrible misunderstanding and they're holding me in Chester. I need you to post bail right away!"

Shock registered on Regina's face. Her body went limp, then she straightened her back, composing herself. If she'd heard those grave words a few hours ago, Regina would have blabbered hysterically, "Locked up! Oh, my God. What for? Listen, don't worry, honey. I'll be there to bail you out as soon as possible." Then she would have run around in confused circles as she tried to get herself dressed and out of the house to go get her falsely accused husband out of jail.

But under the circumstances, after having experienced the shameful disrespect of being informed by her husband's mistress, that he was too busy to take her phone call, Regina could only murmur a sarcastic "Oh really?"

"I know you're upset about that phone call. And I'm going to explain everything later. But right now, I need you to focus. They're holding me on a number of bogus charges—"

"Such as," Regina interrupted. She was close to unleashing all the fury she felt at Matt's indiscretion, but she struggled to keep herself calm so she could hear all the charges.

"Drug trafficking, for one." Matt groaned in disbelief. "Now, you know that's a lie. They're also accusing me of possessing an illegal firearm that was found in the glove compartment of my van. I'm innocent and I can prove it—"

"If I had my way, they'd be adding adultery, also, to the list of charges," she added in an icy tone, which informed him that she held no sympathy for his predicament.

"Don't tell me you're going to start an argument at a time like this!" Matt started inhaling and exhaling, loud and furiously. Finally, he took a calming breath and said softly, "I messed up, baby. I'm sorry." Then his voice took on a gruff, admonishing tone. "But this is not the time for sarcasm, Regina."

"I can't think of a better time," she retorted. "You're having an affair with the young woman who works for you. It's true, isn't it? And your association with her brought about these outrageous circumstances?" she asked in a chillingly calm tone.

"Yes, it's true. But it's over. I swear. I don't want anything else to do with her. Now, can you please focus on the current situation?"

Regina was silent.

Assuming his wife's silence meant she forgave his infidelity since he'd vowed that it was over, Matt began blurting out orders. "First thing tomorrow morning, I want you to get in touch with your credit union. You'll need to get a loan for fifty thousand."

"Your bail is fifty thousand dollars?"

"No, it's three hundred thousand; I only need ten percent to make bail. But I'm going to need a really good attorney to handle these multiple charges. We're probably going to have to pay the attorney at least twenty thousand for a retainer."

"We?" Regina blurted, incredulous. "How dare you involve me in this disgusting mess?" Unable to maintain her cool demeanor or contain her rage, she shook with anger. "The only attorney I plan to pay is a divorce attorney."

"Regina!" Matt bellowed. "This is not the time for you to have a tantrum. Now, get a grip and get focused."

"Get a grip!" she repeated with disdain. "Isn't that what you told me while I grieved for Devon?"

"I grieved, too!"

"We should have mourned the loss of our son together. For ten years I've been trying to get a grip—for your sake. You wanted me to shut off my emotions, get rid of them in the same manner you wanted me to get rid of Devon's things—"

"I didn't think it was healthy to keep his things inside his bedroom as if he was going to come home—"

"It wasn't healthy for you to insinuate that being distraught over the sudden death of my only child was crazy," she shouted. "You were so disapproving, I was forced to box up my feelings, tuck them away, keep my pain out of sight...." Regina's voice cracked with emotion. "All for the sake of not appearing crazy. Well, I acted crazy, anyway. I cried and grieved in the basement. Yes, that's right. Down in the basement with Devon's locked-away toys and clothing, I grieved!" Regina divulged bitterly. "I wept and wailed when you weren't around. Cried out in anguish for as long and as loud as I needed."

"I didn't know..."

"How could you know? You were too busy replacing Devon with your nephew."

"I never..." Matt paused. "I refuse to dignify that accusation. Listen to me, Regina." He spoke in a near whisper. "I was worried about you," he told her in a tone filled with such compassion, Regina hardly recognized her husband's voice. "The amount of time it was taking for you to heal seemed…" Matt faltered. "It seemed like you were taking it too far. I mean, a year or two of grief is understandable, but to be unable to function after a couple of years…well, it's just not acceptable," he said, his voice now mean and filled with disgust, vacant of any tenderness.

"Don't you dare tell me what's acceptable," she screamed at the top of her lungs. "Losing a child is *not* acceptable. It's not!" she wailed.

"Okay, okay, calm down, Regina. Listen, when I get out, we're going to get counseling. Grief counseling—together. We'll see a marriage counselor, too. I'm going to make this right, baby. I promise."

A hard lump formed in Regina's throat. Tears brimmed in her eyes. A few years ago—even a few months ago—her husband's words would have soothed her. Given her hope. But a lot had changed in just the past few hours and Matt's sudden willingness to try to repair their broken marriage was simply too little, too late. She swiped at the tears that streamed down her face and, steadying her voice, she said, "The fact is, seeing me falling apart was too much of a reminder that you'd let our son down."

"It was an accident," Matt yelled. "If you want to point a finger of blame, then you should point it at yourself."

Her eyes widened in disbelief. "How dare you blame me, you bastard!" she shrieked in outrage. If it were possible, she would have reached through the phone line and strangled Matt with her bare hands. Out of the corner of her eye, she saw Cochise shifting his position. Having her private pain, her raw emotions, laid bare was obviously making him extremely uncomfortable, but there was nothing Regina could do about it. She was too far gone to even make an attempt to compose herself.

"I hope you rot in jail," she snarled. "I'm not lifting a finger to help you get out. As far as I'm concerned, you're exactly where you belong. You've got to be out of your mind to ask me to take out a loan for the legal trouble your cheating has caused."

"Don't tell me you're going to punish me forever for one lapse in judgment. It was the first and only time, Regina. In twenty years of marriage, I've been unfaithful only once."

"Only once?" she asked sarcastically. "I've *never* cheated..." Her voice trailed off. She and Cochise hadn't actually had intercourse, but she wondered if their heated foreplay counted as cheating. She supposed it did. Still, her own infidelity would have never occurred had she not found out about her husband's illicit affair. "Matt, our marriage can't be fixed. It's over," she said adamantly.

"You're my wife! Do you want to throw away twenty years over one mistake?" Matt fumed.

Twenty years of loyalty had earned her nothing. Not warmth or compassion. And until only recently, out of some warped sense of duty, she'd been putting up with a sex life that was so bad it was pure torture. Marriage to Matt had not been pleasant. She exhaled, relieved that it was finally over.

"Look, I have to go. Maybe your sister can help you out," Regina suggested.

"My sister can't afford...."

"And neither can I," Regina interjected. "I'll drop your things off at your sister's house in the morning. When you get your next phone call, don't waste it on me—call your girlfriend," she added bitterly.

"Regina!" Matt yelled.

Regina sighed. "Seriously, I'm getting a divorce, so when you do make bail, please don't come here," she warned.

"It's my home, too."

"You're right," she said, letting out a tired sigh. "I'll have my attorney contact you to discuss property division."

Matt shouted, but his words were made inaudible by a loud beeping sound, followed by the dial tone. Regina presumed there was a time limit on Matt's phone call. She gave a mental shrug. *Oh, well.*

Maybe she was bone weary from battling for so long to save a doomed marriage, maybe it was the purging of her feelings regarding the death of her son that caused her to tremble uncontrollably. Whatever the case, overcome with emotion, Regina could not hold back the floodgate of tears. Sniffling and crying and feeling suddenly wobbly on her feet, Regina tottered briefly.

In a matter of seconds, Cochise was off the sofa and at her side, catching her by the arm. He held her in a protective knot as she cried soul-deep, shameless sobs for her lost child—her lost marriage. Cochise held Regina tight until her crying ceased.

Feeling suddenly self-conscious that Cochise had seen her unravel twice in one night, Regina straightened and withdrew from his embrace. "Matt's in jail. He's been arrested on drug charges and possession of a gun. That's all I know right now. I know you said you came back to get a ride back to Chester, so I'll take you." She swiped away residual tears.

"You can't drive tonight," Cochise said firmly. "And I'm not going to leave you here, all alone." His dark eyes were serious.

"I'll be fine." Her voice rose an octave. "Really, I'm fine."

"No, you're not."

"You're right. I'm not," she finally admitted.

"I can't leave you here all alone." He shook his head. "It's against the Recovery House regulations to stay out overnight, but if it's all right with you, I'd like to call the house manager and see if he's willing to bend the rules." Cochise studied her face. "I don't mind sleeping down here on the sofa if you don't have a spare room."

If Cochise was granted permission to stay, he darn sure wouldn't be sleeping on the sofa or in one of her spare rooms. She pictured them together in bed. "Go ahead, make your call." She waved toward the phone she'd just hung up.

Giving Cochise some privacy, Regina went to the kitchen, opened the fridge, and took out a bottle of water. She shoved thoughts of Matt's predicament out of her head. Leaning against the kitchen sink, sipping water, her gaze traveling past the dining room and into the living room where Cochise paced, broad chest bare, with the cordless phone next to his ear.

Her face flushed and her mouth watered. He was such a tantalizing sight. Delicious eye candy! Did she dare hope that such a beautiful, virile man would wind up in her bed, fulfilling her lustful desires for as long as she could stand it?

She watched as he returned the phone to the cradle. *Can you stay?* She searched his face for an answer, but his expression was unreadable. He took slow steps toward her, his eyes downcast. His averted gaze warned her to prepare for a letdown.

Regina turned her back to him and braced herself for the sharp pang of disappointment. Cochise stood behind her, but didn't say anything. "Well?" She intended to sound nonchalant, but the anxiousness in her tone squeaked out. Regina cringed at the sound of her desperation.

"Baby, I ain't going nowhere. I'm staying right here with you," he murmured, turning her toward him, dissolving her humiliation as he wrapped her in his strong arms.

Relief and utter joy washed over her. "I need you," she told him, feeling sexually emancipated. Pulling back a little, she looked at him, her eyes gleaming with raw, carnal lust. "I've never needed anyone like I need you right now."

Her mouth sought his. He dipped his head, meeting her kiss. Cupping her face, Cochise parted her lips with his tongue, stroking her mouth, licking and tasting her with unabashed passion. Yearning welled up inside, and Regina felt herself melting as liquid heat pooled between her thighs.

Time no longer existed. One moment she and Cochise were in the kitchen and in the next moment, they were upstairs, and she was lying naked in her bed with her legs spread. Did she walk upstairs? Did Cochise carry her? And when did she come out of her robe and gown? Her mind was fuzzy as if she'd had too much to drink. With Cochise's head between her legs, his tongue pressed against her clit, she indeed felt intoxicated with pleasure, too disoriented to recall the exact order of events.

Her clit swelled to a hardened bud. Regina thrust forward, seeking more pressure from his tongue. She cried out as if her flesh had been punctured when his tongue left her clit and plunged deeply inside her. She gasped, whimpered, and writhed.

Crouched on the floor at the foot of the bed, Cochise held up her long, shapely legs and probed her sensitive insides with his tongue. She clutched the bed covers and then sat up, her fingers clawing his back. Fearing that in the frenzy of passion, she'd tear the flesh on his smooth, well-muscled back, Regina briefly came to her senses and snatched her hands away.

Acting purely on impulse alone, she leaned back on her elbows and opened her eyes to watch Cochise perform cunnilingus. She couldn't see his expression; his beautiful features were hidden as he buried his face inside her pleasure zone. But what she could see—his silken dark hair spread across her parted thighs—was such a sensual sight, she shuddered and was suddenly overcome by a rush of vertigo. Her heart lurched, the room seemed to spin, her vision dimmed and she fell back heavily, her head flopping against the pillow as she gave in to the swirling sensation that began moving deep inside her groin.

Unimagined pleasure ripped through her, causing her chest to heave. Her nerve ends felt raw, exposed. Then her body began to quake in the wonderful aftershock of the first orgasm she'd ever had that wasn't self-administered. It was the most blissful moment of her life. She felt such peace and fulfillment; she could have easily drifted off to sleep.

Cochise rose from his crouched position. As he climbed onto the bed to lie beside her, she felt his shaft brush against her thigh. In an instant, Regina was aroused and fully alert. She sat up and gazed at the length of his magnificent body as he lay curled next to her on his side. He was indeed a magnificent sight to behold. She ran an appreciative hand along bulging muscles in his back, his shoulders, and his arms. But wanting something else, her hand wandered over his rippled abdominals and caressed a thatch of dark hair beneath his navel. Her curious fingers moved downward toward the muscle that interested her most.

Regina touched Cochise's stiffened manhood and took in a sharp breath. She was briefly paralyzed by the shock of his immense size, then Regina's eyes widened in amazement. Cochise's phallus was alarmingly large, much larger than her battery-operated gizmo. Regina couldn't begin to imagine how many inches the man possessed; he was absolutely, unbelievably humongous.

"It's aiight, baby. I know I'm not built like the average man. It's gonna take a lot of time and patience before I can make love to you the way I want to."

"Uh, I…um…" she stammered idiotically. She could feel her

face flush. She felt awkward and foolish. She'd never performed fellatio. And judging by the girth and length of Cochise's throbbing manhood, she doubted she could accomplish the task without choking to death, and she strongly doubted such a massive member could fit inside her vagina. Having sexual intercourse with this hugely endowed man just didn't seem remotely possible.

"It's aiight," Cochise repeated, as if reading her mind. "What I did—" He paused as he involuntarily licked the lingering taste of her juices from his lips. "I did that for you. I'm cool."

The way his penis quivered and throbbed, the way the veins became pronounced and seemed to pulsate with a surge of yearning, Cochise seemed anything but cool.

Mesmerized by the size and shape of his full throbbing erection, Regina was drawn to it like a magnet. Driven by lust, she lowered her head and allowed her instincts to take over. Her tongue flicked against the smooth, mushroom-capped head. She licked the tip, tasted the salty secretions that oozed out.

"Baby? You sure?" he whispered, and then groaned in defeat when her tongue twirled around the outer edges of his large but perfect cap. Regina covered his shaft with her moist tongue, licking it up and down and moaning as if his sex organ were a large, delicious treat.

She parted her lips, inviting him into her warm, virgin mouth. Cochise slowly eased the head and a few inches of length into Regina's mouth. For a split second, she was shocked by the sensation of having his rigid shaft invade her mouth, but wanting to please Cochise as he'd pleased her, she determinedly sucked on the portion of aroused flesh he'd slid inside her mouth. Surprisingly, she began to enjoy the feeling of his throbbing hardness sliding across her tongue, caressing her gums, hitting the soft insides of her jaws, slipping to the back of her throat, teasing her tonsils.

It was intoxicating—his masculine taste and smell, the husky moans that escaped his lips. When his thrusting movement quickened, Regina braced herself.

"I'm cummin', baby," Cochise uttered, his voice simultaneously breathy and rough. When Regina felt him trying to ease out of her mouth, she began to slurp hungrily, pulling him in and pushing him out in a steady, tantalizing rhythm. His muscles twitched. "I said I'm cummin'," he repeated, urgently fighting against the urge to explode.

Regina held him in place until a gush of passion filled her mouth. It was tangy in taste and had the texture of a milkshake. She swallowed without coercion and then licked her lips, content and certain that she had a newfound acquired taste for Cochise's big dick and his erupting fountain of pleasure.

CHAPTER 20

Onika and the cab driver had watched the brawl between Matt and Nazier in astonishment. After Matt peeled away in his van, Onika ordered the driver, "Pull off!"

"Who's gonna pay me?"

"Pull the fuck off," she shrieked as she saw Nazier stomping toward the car.

By the time the driver finally realized that Onika was in jeopardy, it was too late. Nazier yanked open the passenger door and swung at Onika's head.

"Help!" Onika screamed.

A look of fascination mixed with sympathy filled the driver's eyes as he witnessed Nazier pummeling Onika with violent blows. Fearful of his own safety, he didn't attempt to make a move to rescue Onika from the brutal assault..

"Where that sucka go with my shit?" Nazier demanded, his eyes filled with rage.

"I don't know."

"What the fuck you mean you don't know? That mufucka drove off with my gun and all my shit." Nazier smacked her across the face.

"Stop fuckin' hitting me, Naz. I said I don't know where he went."

"What's his name!"

"Matt Wheeler," she responded before Naz decided to swing on her again. "We live together. He probably went back to the crib." Onika figured if she could get close to home, she could somehow ditch Naz and lock herself inside the safety of her apartment.

"Where at?"

"Uh, we got a place at, um..." She was trying to think of a street close enough to her apartment where she could bail out and not have to run too far, but her mind went blank.

"Oh, now you don't know where you live?"

"I'm trying to think. Damn, I just moved in."

"Yo, where did you pick her up at?" Nazier asked the driver.

"Twenty-Fourth Street," the driver replied without hesitation.

Naz yanked Onika out of the passenger seat, pulled open the back door, pushed her inside, and joined her in the backseat of the cab. "How much she owe you?" he asked while tussling with Onika.

"Thirty dollars," the driver said, craning his neck and staring at the struggling couple in disbelief.

"Aiight, I gotchu." Nazier reached inside one of his pockets and gave the driver a twenty and a ten. "Take us back to her crib and I'll give you ten more when we get there."

The driver nodded. Following Nazier's instructions, he put the car in gear and whizzed down Third Street.

"Ain't you gon' call the cops or something?" Onika shouted to the driver.

The driver steered the cab in silence.

Along with the money, Nazier had also pulled out a pocket-knife. "Shut the fuck up," he warned Onika as he poked her in the side with the sharp end of the knife.

Onika stood at knifepoint outside her apartment door. Her keys clanged as she fumbled to unlock the apartment door. Hopefully, Puddin would be her saving grace. If her friend came out of her drugged haze, Onika figured they could probably overpower and whip Nazier's ass together.

"Puddin!" Onika shrieked the minute she and Naz entered her apartment.

"You callin' that nigga?"

"No, Puddin's a friend of mine. She's 'sleep in the bedroom. Matt must not be home. I didn't see his van parked in the lot."

"Ain't nobody stupid, Onika. Dude probably hidin' in the closet somewhere." Nazier grabbed Onika and put her in a chokehold.

"I ain't lyin'," Onika croaked.

With his arm locked around her neck, Nazier walked Onika around the small apartment, checking all the closets and finally, the bedroom. Sure enough, Puddin was passed out on the air mattress, practically comatose from a megadose of Oxy. Puddin's tongue lolled outside her mouth and slobber dribbled down both sides of her face, dashing Onika's hopes of having assistance in conquering Naz.

"Looks like she's out for the count," he informed Onika with a malicious chuckle. "But she can be dealt with too, if she wakes up looking for trouble." He loosened his grip around her neck and gave Onika a rough shove toward the living room.

"What time is that mufucka gon' get here?"

"Aiight, look. I wasn't being honest with you because I was scared. Real talk, Naz. I ain't bullshitting, Mr. Wheeler don't really live here."

"What?" Nazier reared back, his face set in a murderous scowl.

"He lives somewhere in Philly."

"Where in Philly?"

Onika shrugged.

"Bitch, you was driving that nigga's van, so I know you got a phone number or some kind of way to reach out."

"His number's in my cell phone."

"Call him."

"Can't. I sold my phone."

Nazier pulled out his phone and handed it to her.

"I don't know that man's number by heart," Onika said in a shrill voice.

"Man, this is fucked up." Naz sighed and shook his head in despair. Onika felt hopeful that he would finally give up and take his ass on out of the crib. But instead of going on about his business, Nazier stood with his arms folded, his gaze shifting around anxiously. When his focus landed on the clutter left by the painters, his eyes gleamed with excitement.

"Aiight, then." He dragged the metal folding chair into the kitchen. "Have a seat," he ordered Onika.

"What for?" she asked apprehensively.

Nazier bent down and picked up the cylinder of duct tape.

Instinctively, Onika jerked around and tried to flee the kitchen, but Nazier was quick. He caught her and gripped her by the arm. "Keep fucking with me and I'm gon' yank your arm right out of the socket. Now, sit the fuck down." He slammed her down hard on the chair. "Now, let's see if I can help to refresh your memory," he said as he unraveled the tape.

"Come on, Naz. Don't do me like this. I didn't burn you. I don't even know that old head like that. I just mess with him when I need something. He only comes through the crib every now and then." Onika talked fast and pleadingly, her eyes bulging in fear as Nazier began taping her to the metal chair. She'd had heard stories about people being "duct taped" and had always listened with morbid interest to the harrowing tales of drug deals gone bad, never imagining for a moment that she'd end up in such an unfortunate position. What were her chances of getting out of this alive? Onika searched her memory, trying to recall if any of the duct-taped victims had survived.

Nazier methodically continued taping Onika to the chair. He didn't stop until he'd stripped the last piece of tape from the cylinder. By that time, Onika was cinched so tightly, she could hardly breathe. Through sputtering, choked gasps, she begged for her life. "Please…Naz… don't…kill me. "

"Kill you! Fuck outta here. I ain't tryna get charged with murder." Offended, he grimaced. "But if you don't tell me where you and that nigga got my shit stashed, you gon' wish you was dead."

"Puddin!" Onika croaked. "Wake up! Naz is in here trying to kill me!" She stretched open her mouth and screamed at the top of her lungs.

Nazier drew back his fist and bashed Onika in the mouth. She felt an explosion of pain; her lips swelled up instantly.

"Yo! Why you put me on blast like that?" Naz demanded.

Onika tried to scream but fear locked the sound inside her throat.

"I hope you're happy…putting me through all this bullshit."

Confused, Onika blinked and nodded dumbly.

"Oh, you're admitting you're happy about how that old head played me? That shit's real funny, huh?" Nazier glared at Onika.

Onika quickly shook her head.

"Those packs wasn't cheap, yo. They gotta be replaced. We talkin' big money, yo." He waved his blade in her face.

Blinking rapidly, she shrank back in fear. "I know how you can get your shit back," Onika blurted.

"How?"

"Call my cell," she said thickly. "Tell the dude who bought it off me to look up Mr. Wheeler's number. When you get the number, I can call Mr. Wheeler and tell him to come over—"

"Man," Naz said, dragging out the word in disgust. "You sound like a straight nut. Ain't nobody stupid enough to answer a phone they just bought off a crackhead for five dollars."

Ten, she thought with tremendous regret. If she still had her phone, she'd find a way to push some buttons and scream for help. Onika licked her swollen lips. "Can you take some of this tape from around my arms?" she asked, appealing to Nazier's sense of compassion. "And can you get me some ice from out of the freezer? I gotta put something on my lips," she whined.

Nazier became quiet and thoughtful. "Oh, aiight. I got something for your lips." He stepped behind Onika and moved toward the stove. Turning on a burner, he waved the knife over the flame until the blade was red hot.

"Whatcu doin', Naz?" She turned her head sharply and then hopped up and down, trying to turn the chair around to see what Nazier was up to. She didn't have to wonder long. A few moments later, Naz presented the hot, smoking knife.

The urge to scream was overpowering, but she resisted, knowing a loud outburst would incite Nazier to unspeakable violence. Recoiling, she mumbled in fear, making horrible little sounds of terror.

Nazier brought the smoldering blade close to her face. "Get it together, bitch! Start talkin'."

"I don't know his number. I don't know where he went," she said in a panic, her words muffled by painfully swollen, balloon-like lips.

Nazier swiftly pressed the hot metal against the center of Onika's puffed-out lips and held it there for several agonizing seconds. Too shocked to scream, Onika gasped and shivered violently.

He removed the knife, pulling away a layer of shriveled flesh. Dazed, Onika's eyes rolled into the back of her head.

Nazier slapped her. "Don't pass out on me. Wake up, bitch."

Ghastly moans and garbled words escaped through lips that were so badly burned, the remaining skin stuck together, making her lips appear to be sealed shut. "He went home," she murmured, barely coherent.

"Where your man live at?"

"I don't know."

Using a pant leg, Naz wiped the charred skin off the knife and heated it up again. "Aiight…you ain't talkin'?" he asked as he once again brought the burning blade so close to her lips, she could feel the pulsing heat. "Guess I gotta help refresh your memory."

Fear twisted through her. Onika moaned loudly, trying to awaken Puddin. She screamed for her friend as best she could, but could only manage a hissing sound that slipped through an opening at the corner of her mouth. Nazier set the scorching metal at that spot, burning and sealing off the area where the sound had escaped. He repeated the torturous burning at the other side of her mouth. "Ready to talk?" he asked the semi-conscious woman. When he didn't get a response, Nazier slapped her again, but she remained unresponsive. Frustrated and furious, he kicked the chair, sending it crashing to the floor.

CHAPTER 21

The next morning Regina woke up with a smile on her face. Gazing at her still-sleeping young lover, her smile widened at the memory of the passion and tenderness they'd shared. As she watched the bright sunlight shining on his handsome, chiseled face, Regina accepted last night without regret.

However, the difference in their ages, their life experiences, and the disparity in her and Cochise's financial situations reminded her that it wouldn't be wise to put too much of an emotional investment in this young man's affection.

As if sensing Regina staring at him, Cochise opened his eyes and greeted her with a lazy smile. "Hey, sexy," he said and gave her a flirtatious wink.

She felt at once sensual, beautiful, and young. When was the last time she'd felt like that? Too long ago to remember. After twenty mostly loveless years with Matt, Cochise was just what the doctor had ordered. It wasn't as if she were shopping for another husband.

"What time is it, baby?" Cochise asked.

Baby! Oh, she loved the way he called her baby. Regina sat up. "It's six-thirty," she replied in a casual tone, though her heart was pumping with delight. "I've been awake for a half hour, trying to decide if I should go to work or come back home after I drive you to Chester."

Cochise frowned. "You don't have to take me all the way to Chester. Buses should be rolling by now. Just drop me off at the bus stop on the way to work, aiight?"

"No, I'll drive you. It's not a problem." She patted the top of Cochise's hand. "I doubt if I'd be able to concentrate at work, so I'm going to take the day off. With Matt locked up until Lord knows when, I'm going to need a few days off to go over his business records." Regina sighed. "I have to talk to an attorney and… you know…I just need some time off to gather my thoughts." A crease of worry formed in the area between Regina's eyes. She gazed off into space, trying to prioritize her to-do list, but quickly became overwhelmed. She decided to play it by ear. One step at a time.

"I'd offer to cook you breakfast, but I know you're anxious to give the men their vouchers."

Cochise nodded. "Thanks, I'm straight, though. I don't need breakfast," he said pleasantly. The man was fine as hell and unbelievably well-endowed. He was easy-going and accommodating, he didn't seem conceited or high-maintenance at all.

He hadn't budged from bed, and gave no indication of how soon he needed to get back to Chester. To be honest, Regina wasn't mentally prepared to begin tackling the job of separating her and Matt's finances. Not yet, anyway. What she wanted to do was play hooky from work and spend the entire day in bed with Cochise. She couldn't think of a better time to start getting her walls stretched. She presumed she could take the head and perhaps an inch of shaft. Mmm, the very thought of him pumping his length inside her gave Regina shivers of excitement.

But she couldn't tell him what she was thinking. He'd think

she was a nympho. Regina frowned. Was she? No, she was a late bloomer—a thirty-eight-year-old woman who'd finally experienced a sexual awakening. Hit with the raging hormones of a teenager. The downside to feeling young and sexy was being in a constant state of horniness—having a libido that demanded constant attention. She cut an eye at Cochise and imagined fucking him in every room in her house and in every imaginable position. Her lips curved into a slight smile.

"What's so funny?" Cochise asked, bringing Regina out of her sexual fantasy.

Feigning innocence, she lifted a brow.

"You were deep in thought. Whatever you were thinking about made you smile."

Giving Cochise an honest answer could make her appear too eager—too needy. Realizing the truth could possibly drive him away, Regina responded with the first thought that popped in her mind. "I was smiling as I imagined myself trying to run a business I know nothing about. I have an investment in Matt's business and if I expect to protect my assets, I need to know how the cleaning business works." Regina shook her head. "Maybe you can help me. Matt told me more than once that you were his best worker, and in my current position I sure could use your expertise."

Interested, Cochise sat up. The man was gorgeous. Regina had to drop her gaze for a moment and mentally shake her head. It made no sense for him to look that appealing first thing in the morning. His dark eyes were squinted in curiosity. *Mmm, you better stop looking at me like that.* His jet-black hair was wild and loose. It flowed past his broad shoulders and down to his well-developed chest. *Want some pussy? Say the word and it's yours. I'm willing to deal with the pain.* Aroused, Regina could hardly pull her eyes away from him and assume a business-like persona. "I don't want to lose any of the contracts Matt has," Regina continued, forcing herself to push away all thoughts of sex. "I assume his van's been impounded. That heavy equipment is expensive. I hope nothing happens to it."

Cochise shook his head. "We didn't load anything. Mr. Wheeler never came back with the van. Most of the heavy stuff is still inside the building on Germantown Avenue."

Regina breathed a sigh of relief.

Cochise gave her another serious look. "Like I told you last night, I didn't have the keys, so I couldn't lock up. Everything's probably cool, but I think we should swing by the job to make sure. You're gonna have to get that equipment out of there. You can't hold the company responsible if something turns up missing."

"Move it? How? It won't fit in my car."

Cochise was quiet, pondering. Then he leaned forward. "I have an idea. Can you rent a truck?"

"Sure."

"There you go," Cochise said, nodding. "We'll pick up a van and I'll move everything for you. Where do you store the equipment?"

"Matt keeps some of it in the garage, and some things are kept in the shed at the back of the house."

"Do you have a list of the inventory? You know, the equipment, cleaning products..."

"No, but I'm sure I can find a list. Matt is very meticulous with paperwork."

"Okay, but before you think about trying to run the business, don't you think you should get in touch with the clients and let them know that you'll be handling things temporarily or...you know...until he gets out?"

"You're absolutely right. I hadn't thought abut contacting the clients. Or checking the inventory."

"With both Mr. Faison and Onika out of commission, it might be a good idea for you to cancel the cleaning jobs until you get more help and get things organized."

Regina flinched when Cochise mentioned Onika's name. She wondered if Onika had been arrested with Matt.

"Tell you what. Take me to Chester so I can submit the vouchers and check on Mr. Faison. Oh yeah, I have to let the house manager know what's going on."

Regina frowned. "Do you have to tell him exactly what happened? Can't you just tell him that I'm taking over for Matt? I don't know if I can show my face if everyone knows the whole sordid story. My husband's predicament—his affair with the girl who worked for him is embarrassing."

"I won't give up every detail, but the fact that the boss got arrested is bound to come out sooner or later, especially with Onika involved. I gotta let the men know that it's a strong possibility that we all might be out of work for a while."

"I guess you're right," Regina said wearily.

"The main concern right now is to get the equipment. Mr. Wheeler might get out a lot sooner than you think. If that happens, let him handle his own damage control." Cochise cradled his chin with his thumb and forefinger. "Aiight? So, we're gonna drop off the vouchers, rent the truck, and pick up the equipment. And after that, I guess it would be a good idea to go through his books and find out what's what."

Gratitude tugged at the corners of Regina's mouth, pulling it into a wide grin. Thank God for Cochise. How would she have managed without him?

CHAPTER 22

A bell rang persistently. The sound was muted, but annoying nonetheless. A loud pounding started. Was it in her head? She felt disoriented, couldn't make sense of what was happening. Then the pounding stopped.

Male voices murmured in the distance and then grew stronger. The pounding began again, grew more insistent—*bang, bang, bang*. It seemed like someone was pounding on her head, but she couldn't move her body or turn her head. She couldn't stop the pounding or the aggravating *ding dong* sound that seemed to alternate between poundings. *Oh God, make it stop*, she moaned.

"Regina Wheeler!" a male voice shouted from somewhere in the distance. "Delivery for Regina Wheeler!"

Shuffling, unsteady footsteps approached from behind, responding to the racket, she presumed. Good. Somebody would take care of it. Make it stop. But there was more noise. A blood-curdling scream. "Onika! What the fuck happened?" Puddin shouted and kneeled down to get a look at her friend. "Oh, shit! Who fucked up your lips?" Puddin covered her own mouth in horror. She quickly tried to pick up the chair that Onika was taped to, but Onika was dead weight, resistant to her friend's effort to lift her. Puddin accidentally dropped the chair and screamed again when she heard Onika's head bang against the protrusive edge at the bottom of the refrigerator.

"Ohmigod! I'm sorry, Onika!" Puddin blurted.

A deep gash opened on the side of Onika's head; blood gushed and sprayed Puddin's neck and the front of her T-shirt.

"Somebody, help!" Puddin jumped up and ran screaming to the front door. She swung it open and yelped, shocked that two men stood on the other side of the door.

Startled, the two uniformed men, wearing shirts that read Vanity Furniture jumped when Puddin appeared in the doorway. They gawked at the blood-spattered woman. Taking several steps backward, one of the men, a clipboard in hand, said in a shaky voice, "Delivery, ma'am. We brought your furniture. Is everything all right? Are you Regina Wheeler?"

"Regina who?" Puddin shook her head and waved her hand impatiently. "Look, fuck all that. Somebody tried to kill my best friend. Call an ambulance and call the cops. She's in there dying right now!"

Later, the police took a statement from Onika. She didn't provide them with Nazier's name or whereabouts—doing that would involve court and testifying and risking retaliation from Nazier's peeps. So she claimed she'd been raped, robbed, and brutalized by an unknown, masked assailant.

The hospital treated the burns to her lips and stitched the head wound that had bled profusely but was actually a minor injury, and then released her. But terrified of returning to the apartment and meeting Nazier's wrath again, Onika convinced Puddin that they both needed the protection and drug treatment that the Recovery House offered. Onika was lucky to be alive. She figured after surviving the horror of being duct taped, and after having her lips seared together with a fiery knife, she damn sure deserved a second chance. After the ordeal she'd gone through, there was a strong possibility she'd take her butt to church and turn herself over to the Lord.

Her body ached from head to toe. She thought about getting high one last time, just to dull the pain. But she changed her mind when she thought about the strong possibility of running into Naz. So with Puddin's assistance in holding her up, Onika, the prodigal daughter, limped back to the Recovery House, where both young women were welcomed back into the fold.

Other than a quick head nod, the public defender ignored Matthew Wheeler. He placed his battered briefcase on the table and began to pull out papers. Frowning, he silently glossed over the paperwork, and then gave a huge sigh and turned his focus on Matt.

It was bad enough that Regina wouldn't post bail for Matt, but to find himself looking in the face of an indifferent public defender instead of planning his defense with an aggressive, highly paid, hot-shot attorney was as preposterous as it was for Matt to be behind bars.

"Borrowing a phrase from the street thugs I usually have the honor of representing," the public defender said in a voice thick with sarcasm and arrogance, "that loaded nine-millimeter Glock they found in your possession had a couple of bodies on it."

"Excuse me?" Matt didn't know what the man was talking about. How dare he expect Matt to interpret the language of street thugs. Matt thoroughly detested his lawyer. He intended to dump the incompetent city-paid employee the moment he made bail and could maneuver within the legal system without having to rely on his scornful wife.

"It's been determined that several men were murdered with the gun you had in your possession." The public defender cleared his throat. "Well…that gun is being tied to you. I hate to be the bearer of such bad news, but in addition to the other charges—illegal gun possession, drug possession, and trafficking—you're going to get charged with a murder rap. I have to warn you that your bail is going to be much higher than the original set bail and from the looks of things"—the attorney scowled down at the papers—"you may be standing trial for at least two counts of first-degree manslaughter."

Shocked, Matt stared at the attorney, speechless. Then, the enormity of his words sank in and Matt sprang out of his seat and leaned across the table. Seething, he reached out and collared the smug attorney. "Manslaughter! Are you crazy?" Matt was so furious, he could hardly speak. Spit spewed from his lips as he tried to gather the words to express his shock and rage. "They think I'm a murderer? I don't own a gun, never carried a gun in my life, and I most certainly never killed anyone. Some young punk stole my van and left that gun, the drugs, and any other crap they found in it. The person who committed those crimes is still out there on the loose."

"Guard!" the public defender shouted while trying to break from Matt's iron-clad grasp.

Guards immediately swarmed around Matt. They tussled with him and quickly overpowered and cuffed him.

Kicking and thrashing as he was dragged out of the interview room, Matt bellowed, "Call my wife! I'm being railroaded and I want a real attorney. Do you hear me? Call my wife!"

CHAPTER 23

Cochise fiddled with the radio, scrolling past head-pounding rap music until he found a station that featured R&B and classic soul. "Aw, that's my jawn," Cochise announced, settling back in his seat when smooth male vocals poured from the speakers.

Regina found herself mesmerized by the style of the vocalist.. He reminded her of a modern-day Marvin Gaye. "Who's that?" she asked Cochise.

"That's Raheem DeVaughn. That track is called *Believe*. If I could blow, that's what I'd be singing to you." Cochise smiled and then became quiet so Regina could hear the lyrics.

When the love song concluded, Cochise turned the volume down. "My man was putting it down. He said everything I wish I had the nerve to tell you."

She couldn't help from blushing. It was flattering to know that Cochise was interested in a long-term relationship, but a million unsettling thoughts ran across her mind. "Cochise, there's something I need to ask you."

Giving Regina his undivided attention, Cochise turned the volume down. "Ask."

Regina felt uncomfortable getting all in the man's business, but if she was going to be involved romantically or professionally she would be remiss in not finding out everything she could about the younger man. "What's your addiction, Cochise? How did you end up in the recovery program?"

"I'm addicted to alcohol," he said without hesitation. "Wine, whiskey, beer. You name it, if it could get me drunk enough to numb the pain, I drank it." Sadness softened his tone.

"My girl—my *ex*-girl, Tierra," he went on solemnly, "she wanted to get married. I told her I wasn't ready. She got upset, said I didn't love her. We broke up." Cochise bit down on his lip as if pained by the memory. "It was cool, though. I wasn't ready to make a lifetime commitment. But then I started missing her like crazy. I caved in, called her and told her I was willing to get married if that's what it took to get back together.

"She started planning a big, elaborate wedding. Preacher, church, family and friends, the whole nine. But I wasn't with all that. Being stubborn, trying to have my way because I felt like I was being forced into something I wasn't ready to do, I told her if we didn't have a small, private ceremony at City Hall, then we could just call the whole thing off." Cochise paused and lowered his head as if he were too overcome with emotion to speak.

"If this is too uncomfortable..."

"No, no. It's cool. I need to talk about it," he said, nodding. "Tierra wanted to get married so bad she went along with it, but on the day we were supposed to get married, she insisted we drive our separate cars. She didn't want me to see her in her wedding dress, said it would be bad luck." Cochise inhaled, drawing in a deep breath, gathering himself before he continued. "Tierra never made it. She was killed in a car crash. A head-on collision. Blaming myself, I started drinking. I drank so much, I was hospitalized for alcohol poisoning. And that's when I finally realized that my drinking was going to kill me. I decided I wanted to live. The social worker at the hospital told me about the Recovery House."

"How long have you been sober?"

"A year and a half. But I'm not gon' hold you, it's still a struggle. Every day is a struggle."

Regina thought about her addiction to designer bags. Unlike a drug, alcohol or gambling addiction, her spending was controllable. She didn't neglect bills or go without food. But she could relate to the need to numb the pain of loss with some form of overindulgence.

Stopping at a red light, Regina reached over and touched Cochise's hand. When the light changed, she pushed down on the gas pedal. "Matt and I lost our son," she said softly, keeping her eyes on traffic. "His name was Devon."

"I'm sorry to hear that. How long ago?"

"It's been ten years now."

"What happened? Was your son sick?"

"No." Driving through traffic, Regina was catapulted back in time. Taking in a breath, she composed herself. "He drowned," she said in a monotone, detaching herself emotionally in order to speak the unspeakable. "Devon drowned when he was seven years old. His father bought him a fishing rod and promised to take him on a fishing trip. Matt cancelled when his job offered him overtime to work the weekend. Devon was so disappointed, he had a tantrum. Cried and wouldn't go outside to play with his friends. I felt like I was being punished by his constant crying, whining, and moping around the house all day Saturday. By Sunday, I was so weary of his sullen disposition and so angry with Matt for leaving me to deal with it, I yelled at Devon and insisted that he go outside and play in the backyard. Every fifteen minutes, I checked on him. But when I called him in for lunch, he didn't answer. After scouring the neighborhood looking for him, I gave up and called Matt. He came home and we called the police. Devon's body was found in a nearby creek. He'd secretly taken his fishing rod out of the backyard shed and decided to go fishing by himself."

Surprisingly, Regina didn't cry. Speaking of the tragic details of her son's death was therapeutic. And for the first time, she no longer pointed the finger of blame at Matt or herself. Neither could have known that their decisions that weekend would alter their lives forever.

Regina and Cochise made the rest of the trip to Chester in silence. No radio, no conversation. The mood, however, was not tense. Regina and Cochise were both pensive—silently in awe that two wounded souls had found each other, knowing that together their wounds would heal.

Matt's alleged drug trafficking and the murder charge were hot topics in the small town of Chester. The story made the front page of the local newspaper, Cochise discovered when he dropped off the vouchers at the Recovery House. There was, however, a bit of good news. Mr. Faison had his medication and was doing fine. And he'd heard that Onika had returned to the womens' Recovery House, vowing to stay clean.

Most likely, the story wouldn't hit the bigger newspapers in Philadelphia, so Cochise kept quiet about Matt's situation being splashed on the front page of *The Delaware County Daily Times.* That information would undoubtedly upset Regina, and what she didn't know wouldn't hurt her. Right now, he wanted her to focus on getting the costly equipment out of the job site and safely to her home.

After Regina rented the truck, Cochise drove the U-Haul, picked up the equipment, and returned it to Regina's home.

Back at the Wheeler household, Cochise and Regina pored over Matt's records. There was one alarming discovery after another, the first being that Matt was several months behind in payments to numerous cleaning product suppliers. Each had sent threatening letters with dates when the account would be suspended. Also startling was the fact that over four thousand dollars in furniture had been charged to one of Matt and Regina's joint credit cards. But the most shocking discovery of all was the sight of Matt's signature on the lease to an apartment in Chester.

So stunned was she by the depth of her husband's deception, Regina was too numb to feel any emotion. However, when the fax machine in Matt's office began spitting out a slew of cancelled contracts, Regina was finally able to feel something. Fury!

"Apparently, Matt's troubles are public knowledge. How could he allow his affair to get him into such a mess?" She stared at one of the faxed pages and handed it to Cochise. "His drug-related legal troubles are in direct violation of his agreement with the Recovery House; all the businesses he contracted with have pulled out," she added as she watched Cochise peruse the faxed messages. "I just can't believe Matt has gotten himself into such a terrible financial mess, not to mention the criminal charges."

"I don't think Mr. Wheeler is guilty of those charges. I didn't want to upset you, but everybody's talking about it at the Recovery House...that gun they found on Mr. Wheeler was used in a murder—"

Regina mouth dropped open but not a sound came out. "Murder?" she finally asked.

Cochise nodded. "I don't want to lose you," he said softly, "but if you still love your husband and want to stand by his side, I definitely can understand it. The things he did—cheating on you with Onika, splurging on dumb stuff when he should have been handling his business, well…that shit was slimy, but I don't think he deserved to take the fall for crimes he didn't commit."

"After twenty years of marriage, I'd be lying if I said I didn't care about Matt."

Though he maintained an impassive expression, Cochise's heart was beating fast as he listened to Regina, waiting to find out the fate of their relationship.

"I'm furious with Matt, but I'm not letting my anger determine my actions. I'm going to help him. I'll take out a second mortgage on the house if that's what it takes to afford a good defense attorney, but I want a divorce. I'm not in love with my husband. Our marriage was over years before he began the affair with Onika. Our marriage started dying when we lost our son and neither of us knew how to revive it."

Regina looked so sad, Cochise embraced her. "You know I'm here for you. Just tell me what you need."

Frightened, exhausted, and love deprived, Regina looked up at Cochise. "Right now, all I need is you."

CHAPTER 24

Two weeks later, Onika Brandt, now holy and sanctified, stood up to give a testimonial during a special celebration for the men and women who had successfully completed a week or more of sobriety. Her brush with death, she recounted, had turned her life around. Onika's testimonial soon turned into a full-fledged praise service.

Onika spoke with passion of her nightmarish encounter with an alleged unknown assailant. "I was a sinner. Chasing after drugs, I turned my back on my heavenly Father and ran smack into the arms of Satan," she said, mimicking the posture and vocal quality of an evangelical minister. "But the devil didn't win!" Onika shouted. "Oh no," she said, shaking her head dramatically. Lowering her tone, she continued, tears streaming down her cheeks, "I turned my back on the Lord, but I'm standing here today because the Lord didn't turn his back on me."

Thundering applause amidst a chorus of "Amen" and "Thank you, Jesus," erupted inside the small room where the recovering addicts took turns recounting the experiences that had made them hit rock bottom and finally seek help.

After Onika's testimonial, Cochise pulled her aside to speak to her privately.

"Glad to see you're getting yourself together."

"Thanks," she said, licking nervously at her scarred lips.

"Me and you never got along, but there was never any real beef between us, right?"

"Right," she murmured cautiously.

"Good, just trying to make sure we're cool and everything."

Onika nodded. Cochise could tell that his sudden show of friendship made her uneasy.

"So…um, I guess you heard about Mr. Wheeler."

"Yeah, it's a shame the way things went down." She lowered her eyes and ran a nervous hand through her hair.

Cochise gave Onika a long, knowing look. "Oh, so you're not going to say anything? You're just gonna sit back and let the man take that fall?"

"I don't know what—"

"You know what I'm talking about. I guess turning your life around, being all holy and sanctified, is just a front." His harsh tone and expression challenged her.

Onika backed up a little. "I ain't have nothing to do with—"

"Right now, you're like a celebrity around here, but when I tell everybody about your role in bringing an innocent man down…" Cochise shook his head ominously. "You think they still gonna be singing your praises when they find out you're covering up for a drug dealer?"

Onika looked pained. Her body sagged. "You don't understand. If I give him up, him and his peoples gon' come after me. The next time that nut pulls a knife out, he's gon' be using the sharp end…poking a bunch of holes in my ass."

"You know you're safe here. We're not gonna let nobody harm you."

"But I'm scared," she whined.

"The program will stand behind you and you know it. You

need to give the police some information. Mr. Wheeler is facing hard time and you know that's not right. If you love the Lord the way you claim to, you'll do what's right." He patted Onika on the shoulder, then turned around and told all his friends goodnight.

Cochise was now an employee of the Recovery House. He no longer resided there. Regina had inherited Matt's debts and was required to pay the rent on the apartment for the duration of the one-year lease as well as make payments on the furniture her husband had purchased with their joint credit card, so at Regina's request, Cochise moved into Onika's former apartment in Chester. Conducting their love affair on neutral turf instead of Regina's and Matt's home seemed the most respectful thing to do.

All the fight was gone. Having been behind bars for almost three weeks, Matthew Wheeler was no longer hostile and combative toward his wife. Looking into her husband's eyes, Regina saw only remorse and shame.

"I' going to use the house as collateral to pay your bail, but I think we should discuss selling the property."

"Why do you want to sell it?"

"Sad memories. It's time to move forward," she said solemnly. "But on the bright side, I've found an attorney, a very expensive attorney. I'm using half the money from the sale of the house to pay his fee. I think it's fair that you and I split the rest of the money."

Matt lowered his head and nodded. "I'm so sorry, Regina."

"I know you are." Regina pondered briefly. "Matt," she said softly.

Matt looked up.

"Onika Brandt has agreed to come forward; she's going to testify at your trial. Her testimony is critical to your release."

"You spoke with Onika?" Matt looked dumbfounded that his wife would willingly have a civil conversation with his ex-mistress.

"No, not directly. Langston Belgrave—Cochise—convinced her to come forward."

"How do you know Cochise?" There was an undercurrent of jealousy in Matt's tone. His apologetic expression disappeared.

Regina saw no reason to tell Matt the whole story, so she told him as much as she wanted him to know. "He helped me move your equipment. Without his assistance, I don't know what I would have done." Regina paused, breathed in deeply. "Cochise is really ambitious and has a strong desire to run his own commercial cleaning business. He was able to form a partnership with the Recovery House. He got a small business loan, and because I needed cash to pay the attorney's retainer, I sold him the equipment. Somewhere along the way, Cochise and I became involved."

Matthew gripped his head in agony. "How could you do this to me, Regina? Cochise is too young for you and he's one of my—"

Regina abruptly rose to leave. "I didn't come here to argue, Matt. I can't understand how you have the nerve to feel slighted. If Cochise is too young for me, why was twenty-year-old Onika just the right age for you?"

Matt didn't flinch, demonstrating his belief in a double standard. "That man worked for me. I didn't disrespect you by cheating on you with one of your friends." Matt laughed bitterly and shook his head. "Cochise! Who would have thought that lowlife alcoholic could steal my wife and my business?"

"He's a recovering alcoholic," Regina said, defending Cochise.

"You told me they were *recovering* addicts when you hired them to work for you," she reminded Matt. "Let me remind you of something else. It was your infidelity that caused you to lose your wife and your business." She sighed and looked deeply into his eyes, wanting the severity of her words to penetrate. She was also curious to see if she felt some vestige of the love she'd once felt. But there was nothing. No lost love to salvage or recapture. "It's over between us, Matt. Accept it."

CHAPTER 25

Inside Cochise's apartment, Regina prepared dinner wearing a sheer gown. She listened to slow jams as she sliced and diced an array of colorful ingredients. The table was set to create an ambience of elegance and romance with lighted candles and a centerpiece of delicate cut flowers. At the stove, Regina heated extra-virgin olive oil in a sauté pan, adding crushed garlic, onions, and red peppers.

Cochise arrived home to the appetizing aroma, but the moment he saw Regina, he felt the jolt of a different type of desire. Stirring ingredients, she turned around and greeted her man with a smile. Cochise walked up behind her and kissed the back of her neck, inhaling her scent. He reached over and turned off the burner. "Dinner smells good, but you smell better." He picked her up and carried her to the bedroom.

Regina didn't resist. Dinner could definitely wait. Tonight was the night that Cochise would possess her. Tonight she intended to allow Cochise to fill her with all his thirteen inches.

Cochise slipped off the straps of Regina's gown and peeled it off; the soft fabric fluttered down to the floor. "You're beautiful, baby," he said while hungrily gazing at her naked, curvaceous form.

From her prone position on the bed, Regina watched Cochise

strip out of his shirt. Seeing him bare-chested with his rippling muscles exposed was so tantalizing, Regina had to restrain herself from leaping up and worshipfully caressing each isolated muscle.

When he slid down his jeans and stepped out of them, Regina took in a sharp breath. She watched as Cochise hooked his thumbs under the waistband of his boxers and pulled them down. The beauty of his physique took her breath away. Her body tensed, her mouth watered at the sight of his enormous phallus. His face, his body, his dick...gorgeous! Way too much eye candy, the sugar rush made her head spin.

He straddled her, lowered his head, and kissed her. His lips felt soft against her own. Regina parted her lips, inviting him to plunge his tongue inside and explore her mouth. Tasting each other was incredibly sensual, Regina moaned and Cochise made a small groaning sound in the back of his throat.

Abruptly he pulled his mouth away and covered her breasts with his lips. Murmuring husky sounds of pleasure, Cochise moved down and squeezed her luscious orbs together, teasing her twin peaks with his tongue, sending the hardened pearls hot sensations that quickly traveled down to the core of her womanhood. Arching her back and twisting with raw desire, Regina cried out. Her sounds of passion blended with the music that played in the background.

On cue, Cochise abandoned her breasts and moved to the bottom of the bed where he repositioned Regina, pulling her clenched thighs apart, spreading them wide and drawing up her knees. With her labia separated, her pinkness on display, Cochise dipped his head. "You gotta pretty pussy," he whispered, his hot breath tingling against her moist, rose-colored flesh. He inserted a spiraling finger. When her juices began to flow, he cupped her round behind and lifted it until her hot moisture met his lips.

Enraptured by the smell of Regina's feminine scent, Cochise pushed his tongue inside, taking in her flavor, a tasty combination of tangy and sweet. He grazed her clit with his teeth and then proceeded to lick, suck, and eat her as if he were a starving man and her pussy, a scrumptious entrée.

As good as Cochise was making her feel, Regina pulled back. She didn't want to reach an orgasm with oral sex. "Stop," she whispered urgently. "I'm ready, Cochise."

By the look of Cochise's erect penis, the head glistening with pre-cum arousal, Regina knew it would be easy to convince her lover to penetrate her deeply, to give her every inch of his length.

He gave her the smooth slippery head of his dick and then slowly pulled it out. He looked down at her questioningly. "More," Regina uttered. But instead of penetrating, Cochise held his dick in his hand and slid it up and down her silky, warm entrance. Regina arched again and opened her legs wider, crying out, pleading for more. He penetrated again, this time pushing in deeper, looking at her intently and gauging her expression as he pulled out his steely rod. Her eyes demanded more. Easing in his thickness past the halfway point, Cochise stopped when he felt her tightness close around him. Concerned, he looked down at her, gauging her expression to estimate her ability to take more. Beads of perspiration trickled down Regina's face.

"You okay, baby?" Cochise asked.

"Yes." The word was spoken in a blissful whisper.

"I don't want to hurt you."

"I need you." Regina's voice was low and throaty. She raised her hips, demanding his sex.

Unable to resist her command, he drove his pulsing male blade halfway and then stopped. "Are you all right?"

Panting, she nodded.

His breathing ragged, and his skin damp with sweat, Cochise gave Regina slow pumps at first. Then surrendered to the pain of his aching hardness, he plunged deeper, widely separating her silky folds as he burrowed himself into her warmth..

Regina screamed as she met his thrusts, the sound was a combination of pleasure and pain. Soon, Cochise could feel her walls expanding. Her hips rotated in acceptance. His huge erection slid in without resistance, as their hungry bodies ground against each other.

She had all thirteen inches of her man's thick length planted deeply, and the feeling of his hot flesh threatened to drive her over the edge. She wrapped her legs around his waist, pulling him closer as she gave in to the building waves of ecstasy that crested within.

Cochise's breathing quickened as he felt Regina's clenching spasms. Abandoning himself to the pleasure he'd denied himself for so long, he thrust in and out, unafraid of showing his emotions as he moaned her name. Cochise gave a harsh groan of masculine surrender as he released his hot seed. Bringing his lips close to Regina's ears, he whispered, "I know it's too soon to be talkin' like this, but I can't help it. I'm in love. Can we take this to the next level?"

Regina clung to him and buried her head against his massive shoulder. For far too long, she'd gone without passion and love. Silently, she vowed to never take him for granted; she'd cherish the love he offered forever.

"I love you, too," she whispered, feeling completely safe in letting him know how she felt.

"Baby," Cochise murmured. "I can't believe you were able to

handle my size like that. I thought it would take a couple of months to stretch you out."

"I'm shocked, too. But you know what they say...Love conquers all." Regina suppressed a smile. One day she'd tell her big, gorgeous man the real story. Impatient to feel every inch of his sex, she'd sped up the stretching process by purchasing a giant-sized, sex toy.

It was money well spent, but her new gizmo and her other fake dick were both going straight into the dumpster. She reached over and stroked Cochise's flesh. His thirteen inches quickly rose to the occasion, confirming that Regina would never again have to rely on battery-operated sex.

ABOUT THE AUTHOR

Allison Hobbs is a national bestselling author of *Pandora's Box*, *Insatiable*, *Dangerously In Love*, *Double Dippin'*, *The Enchantress*, *A Bona Fide Gold Digger*, *The Climax* and *Big Juicy Lips*. Her next books are *Disciplined*, a Quickiez title and part of the Invitation Erotic Odyssey series; *Pure Paradise*, and *The Sorceress*. She lives in Philadelphia, Pennsylvania where she is working on her next novel. Visit the author at www.allisonhobbs.com